Wielder
Volume one

Wielder

Volume one

The Power Manifestation Arc

Morgan Barnard

ISBN: 9798425691125

Trigger warnings for Wielder Volume one:
Child abuse – verbal, emotional, and mentions and implications of physical
Religious trauma – mentions
Emotional manipulation
Abusive behaviours and kidnapping

Tiktok: @mb.disconnected
Twitter: @Disconnected_E
Instagram: @disconnected.entertainment
YouTube: Disconnected Entertainment

DEDICATION

I dedicate this book to you. You reading this book right now. By reading Wielder you are helping me achieve my dream of sharing stories with the world, so thank you.

CONTENTS

ACKNOWLEDGMENTS

This book would never have happened without the help of my friends and family, without their support and love I never would have been able to push through and finally complete my first book. My mother, Sarah Barnard, and my close friend, Michael, helped me to edit this book and for that I will be forever grateful.

BookTok and AuthorTok also helped to keep me motivated, seeing all the other indie authors going through the process together always kept me inspired. Never underestimate the power of the internet.

CHAPTER ONE
First Steps

Rain lashed down onto Daniel Andrew's face, harsh and cold, but it didn't bother him. He had run in worse. He ran every day; the weather was no excuse to slack off. With his shorts just above his knees and his hoodie pulled as far as it would go over his head, Danny only sped up, pushing himself as far as he could. Being stronger, faster, meant that he could help more people, something that he had not been able to do in the past.

The impact on his knees as his feet slammed against the ground broke his train of thought every so often, but pain would never stop him, it would only ever make him more determined to keep moving forward as that small voice in his head screamed at him that it didn't matter. What had happened to her, he could never let that happen, not to her, or anyone else. Never again.

A deafening crack of thunder made Danny slow down and look up from the floor, watching the splashes from his feet fall back to the path. As he did, he saw a man standing over a young woman. It was dark, and he couldn't see her face properly, but she was holding her arms close to her chest and she kept shuffling her feet away from him. He could not stand people using their power to stand over others, he found it cowardly and one of the lowest things that a person could do. The fight should always be fair.

With a deep glare on his brow, Danny took out his earphones and walked over to them.

"Hey," he called out as he approached them, "Miss, are you okay?"

The young woman didn't speak, she just looked up at him. She looked uncomfortable, which told him all he needed to know. The man looked annoyed, but his feelings were not important. Danny had stepped in to stop him. He had learned the hard way that even if the situation does not involve you, if you do nothing, you are still letting it happen. He was just a kid then, but now he could do something, now he could step in and help where he could. No one would be hurt the way Lilith was, not while he was there.

"We're fine," the man said, taking a step towards the young woman.

Danny gritted his teeth and stepped up to the man, looking up at him through his dripping wet, blonde hair. "I don't remember asking you anything."

The man laughed a little as he looked down at Danny's irritated expression. "You need to mind your manners, kid."

"And you need to back off," Danny snarled, clenching his fists as he stood toe to toe with the man. For a moment he studied Danny's expression a little to see if he was serious about where this was going. He didn't have time to finish his assessment of Danny before he got a punch to the face as Danny swung for him.

"You picked the wrong fight, asshole!" The man shouted as electricity sparked around his hands

Danny placed himself in front of the young woman to try and protect her, "I'm Danny by the way. Stay behind me please."

"Rachel," the young woman said shakily, stepping back to get away from them.

With his hands up to protect his face, Danny darted forward. He hit out, catching the man in the jaw again. A sharp pain stung his side.

The man had got a hit in under his defenses. Danny's side burned as he slammed his knee into the man's hip, kicking hard against the man's leg, forcing Danny back a little. Without thinking, Danny wound up to punch the man again, but he seemed to have the same idea. Their fists collided, letting electricity flow through both their arms, making burn marks across Danny's skin.

Danny yelled in pain as he held his right arm close to his chest, he checked quickly behind him to make sure that Rachel was okay. She looked scared but she didn't seem hurt. Looking back to the fight, Danny could see the man moving his arms to channel the electricity flowing from them. His movements allowed it to travel along his skin and through his fingers without burning him the way it had burned Danny.

"Do you know what he's doing?" Rachel asked, reaching out for Danny's arm.

"I'm gonna guess magic," Danny replied with a determined smile, trying to make her feel better. He had not seen this kind of magic before. What Lilith had been able to do was like dark shadows, or smoke. He did not even fully know if what Lilith could do was magic. It was just what they had called it when they were kids.

"Magic?" Rachel asked, pulling her arm back, afraid, "can you do that too?"

"No."

Distracted by talking to Rachel, Danny didn't see the man throw electricity towards him. In a sudden burst of bravery, Rachel reached for Danny, throwing them both to the ground. Danny scraped his knee across the tarmac, but he was grateful that he had not been hit with whatever kind of blast the man had sent towards him.

"We should run," Rachel told him, his blue jumper clenched tightly in her fists. She looked terrified. She was glad Danny was there, but she was losing hope in her white knight after his opponent had revealed that he had superpowers.

"We can't run away from a fight," Danny frowned, pushing himself back up so that he was ready to fight again, "he needs to be stopped."

"You're out of your depth, we both are," Rachel tried to reason with him, tugging at his jumper to try and get him to run with her. He was strong, she could tell that with every tug at his jumper. He barely moved. But strength meant nothing when the person you are fighting can kill you without touching you.

Danny paused for a moment, then launched forward to get them both out of the way of the man's second attack. The ground where they had just been, flew into the air and showered down on top of them. They both sat for a second just looking at the hole that was now in the path.

"You should really listen to her," someone said, causing all three of them to look round.

The voice came from a boy, clearly much younger than all of them. His hair was blonde and flowing around his head as electricity sparked around him. His clothes were tight on him and rubber looking. He wore bulky boots and a jacket that was burning up as the sparks caused scorches and fire in the fabric.

"You are seriously out of your depth."

CHAPTER TWO
Dex

The boy stood, his jacket burning away from his suit, staring at the man that had attacked Danny and Rachel with an intense look. His hair flying around his head as though it was caught in a strong wind. He seemed calmer than the man who had attacked them, more controlled. Electricity bounced from the path causing small stones to fly into the air as it wound its way through the air and around his limbs and fingers. The boy shifted his weight, ready to fight. He moved his right leg behind him to stabilize himself, the frown on his brow only accentuated the focused look in his eyes.

"Lumin thinks you're ready, aye?" The man laughed, set his shoulders, and braced his feet. He looked amused by the boy; his cocky attitude written all over his face. "How old are you now anyway? Like twelve?"

"Old enough to beat your ass," the boy spat, launching himself forward. A bright light shot from the boy's hands in strands that broke away and reformed as they travelled in front of Danny's eyes. He knew that it had happened in merely a matter of seconds, but as Danny watched it pass in front of him, it felt as though he could see every spark of electricity that flew through the air in slow motion. Clearly having been overconfident, the man had obviously severely underestimated the power of the boy. The electricity hit him so hard it sent him flying back through the air, slamming him into a tree behind him.

"Jesus, Dex," the man grunted as he pushed himself up off of the floor, "someone's been at the punching bag."

"Yes, that is the point of training," Dex said in a bored tone as he walked over to the man, his power still sparking around him.

Before the man could get back to his feet, Dex sent another blast towards him, keeping him down while he closed the gap between them. In a blink of an eye, Dex seemed to turn into a blur and then reappear closer to the man, who had crumpled up into a ball after the second hit. Danny rubbed his eyes, thinking he must have gotten something in them to make his vision go blurry for a second. But everything he was seeing was strange, so he didn't know what he was supposed to think anymore. Was he supposed to think everything was magic? Or was he supposed to think that his eyes were dry and blurring his vision like any other normal person would?

"You're under arrest," Dex spoke softly as he leaned over the man, bending his knees to crouch. It was loud enough for Danny to hear, because he was looking eagerly over to where the two of them had been fighting.

"Good luck with that," the man hissed, swinging for Dex, his fist lit up, engulfed in electrical currents.

To their surprise, Dex was unfazed. He simply clasped the fist in his own hand, conducting the electricity through his own body as it sparked away from his suit and skin. Danny stood in awe as he watched the two of them. Dex's eyes were a bright white, glowing like lightning. He couldn't believe what he was seeing. He had never seen magic like this before. The world he thought he had known his whole life was suddenly expanding infinitely. Before, he had believed in only one type of secret magic and even then, he had only ever seen one person do it. Lilith was his only example of this side of the world. He, like everyone else, assumed that the videos and pictures of this sort of thing on the internet were edited, faked. He thought he had wrapped his head around it. He thought he was brave enough to face it. To save her. To find her. But right now, he was the most scared he had ever been. Danny could not deny the reality that there were several occasions on which he could have died, if the man had not thought less of him for not having magic, he would likely be dead. And if this Dex boy had not shown up and saved them both, then he could have died then as well. All he could do now was wish that this Dex boy was one of the good guys and was not going to kill them both for what they had seen.

As Danny was experiencing his crisis, Dex was about ready to finish the fight that he had dominated since the first blow. With his free hand, he pulled back and redirected the electricity that was flowing through him into his fist and struck the man cleanly, knocking him unconscious. Relaxing, Dex let go of the man's hand and stood up from his crouching position. Silently, he took something small out of a pocket on the side of his boot, with a swift shake it turned into a pair of handcuffs. Dex bent down again and placed the cuffs on the man's wrists, making sure he was securely restrained.

Danny edged forward to get a better look as Rachel clung to his arm, tugging at him to get him to stay back, but her efforts were in vain. As he watched from behind a bush a little bit away from where Dex was, Danny saw the cuffs expand to cover the man's hands fully, pressing them tightly together so that he would not be able to move them when he woke up.

'If he could wake up,' Danny thought. He found it hard to believe that anyone would be able to survive after one hit like that, let alone three. Still, it did not seem too large a leap for him to believe that the man was still alive, this Dex boy seemed very controlled from what Danny had seen, and the way he was acting indicated to Danny that Dex was sure that the man was still alive.

Rachel and Danny flinched back a little when Dex stood up again. He had not seen them crouched behind the bush as he looked back to check on the civilians he had left on the curb while he dealt with the man. On most of his missions though, if civilians were involved, they tended to run away as soon as they could, so the fact that they were no longer on the curb did not surprise him in the slightest. There was a rustle in the foliage next to him which caused him to swing his head around rather suddenly, causing a twinge in his neck that made him wince a little, but he tried his best not to show it.

"I'm sorry you had to witness that," Dex had quite a young voice when he was calm. It took Danny back a little. He seemed to have forgotten how young he looked the first time they had seen him that evening. It was hard to imagine such power coming from such a young man.

"I didn't see you take any videos, but we can't be too careful as people tend to be scared of what they don't understand," Dex told them, holding his hands out gently as he spoke, "may I see your phones?"

Too scared to speak after what they had both just seen this young man do, Danny and Rachel both handed Dex their phones out of their pockets immediately and without question. Dex barely even looked at them as he held them, there was a small spark and both phones lit up as though they had received a notification as they lay in the palms of his hands.

"That should do it," Dex said with an apologetic smile as he handed the phones back to the two of them. "I'm sorry if I broke them."

He gave them a final, awkward, nod before turning and walking away from them. Making his way back to stand over the man, he took his own phone out of his pocket. He spoke for a couple of minutes before hanging up the phone and putting it back into his shoe, simply to stand motionless next to his criminal.

CHAPTER THREE
Where Is She?

There were a few minutes where they all stood in silence before a small group of people made their way into the park, three of them, all wearing black suits. Even their shirts were black, making it hard to make out if they were wearing ties or not. They walked calmly over to where Dex was standing, he seemed distracted, but he looked up once they got close. Dex didn't seem to even say a word to them, he simply glanced down at where the man was and then walked away after one of them handed him a grey cap with a lightning bolt on the front. He sighed as he looked down at the burnt remnants of his jacket on the floor, he had forgotten to take it off. He would have to walk back like this but at least his job was done. He finally relaxed properly, letting the tension out of his shoulders, and stretching a little. Doing those moves took a lot out of him, the amount of electricity he had to produce as well as the channeling of the man's attack, he was tired and just wanted to get home.

Danny had been in too much shock to do anything; he had just been soaking up all the new information that had been presented to him up until then. Nothing could've prepared him for what just happened. He could never know if he would still have helped if he had known about the powers the man had. He would certainly like to think that he would have, but there was no way he could gauge how brave he would have been. That thought was going to nag at him for a while. He hadn't quite wrapped his head around all of it yet, but he couldn't let Dex get away without at least trying to talk to him.

"Hey!" Danny called out, jogging away from Rachel after prying his arm out of her hands as she tried to cling onto him, "Wait! Who are you?"

Pausing for a second, Dex looked back to see who was calling him, but he didn't stop to talk; he simply turned away and kept walking without a word. He had been quite glad when he thought that the two of them had run away, it made his job a lot easier. Dex didn't like people that asked questions, there wasn't a book or instructions on what he could say and what he was not supposed to reveal. He knew that he should keep his powers as secret as he could but, after what they had seen, do the rules even still apply? The boy had held his own against his opponent for a short amount of time at least, was he supposed to investigate that, what if he needed help? Or he could just be stronger than he looks. Then it was none of his concern and he should keep walking. Lumin had always told him to mind his business, so that is what he was going to do.

"Wait," Danny called after him as he caught up to Dex, "what was that? Listen, I just have a couple of questions."

"I can't tell you anything, I'm sorry," Dex said, trying to get Danny to leave him alone so that he could go home. His arms were starting to ache, and he really wanted to get to sleep, he did not have the time to be overthinking about matters that had nothing to do with him.

"Please, I've been looking for someone, for a long time," Danny tried to explain himself as quickly as he could as he lengthened his stride to keep up with Dex who was surprisingly fast for someone significantly smaller than he was, "I think she's like you. She could do... things and there was an accident a long time ago and someone like your friends over there came and took her away, so please if you know anything, I need your help."

Dex stopped walking abruptly, causing Danny to almost walk into him. He sighed as he gave in to Danny's pleading. If he already knew about this stuff, then there couldn't be much harm in filling him in on some of the details. "Does she have a name?"

"Her name's Lilith Romano," Danny explained, happy to have some cooperation, "she wasn't exactly like you but, I figure you could help me because I bet you know more than I do. She could do things, but not with the lightning stuff that you can do. She could make smoke and these little animal things."

Dex sighed, he tried not to be annoyed because he knew that Danny just didn't understand but, he was tired and did not want to explain the ins and outs of the wielding community to a civilian that barely knows of its existence. "Your friend and I, we're not the same. We do very different things. From what you've said, she's probably a shadow wielder, I am an electricity wielder. We tend to stick with our own. I'm sorry, but there is no way I could or would have known her."

"But-" Danny started but Dex raised his hands to stop him.

"Listen, I can't help you," Dex told him, "I'm sorry about your friend, but she's probably in good hands if that's any consolation."

"I need to find her," Danny's voice softened as he spoke, the desperation was no less but Dex could hear that the hopefulness was wavering, "I couldn't help her before, and I can't help her now if I don't know where she is. Please."

"I can't help you," Dex told him again, taking a step away from him, "you should go home, and make sure your other friend gets home safe too."

Danny glanced back to where Dex had gestured. Rachel was standing behind them. She was still shaken up by the whole ordeal and did not want to go anywhere alone. Danny gave a nod and walked the couple of steps it took to get back to her. Once he was satisfied, Dex turned and continued to walk in the direction he was originally going. Danny stood and watched Dex walk away from them, it felt like the one lead he had had since he had lost her all those years ago was slipping through his fingers. In all honesty, he had mostly given up on trying to find Lilith. It had been so long; he probably wouldn't even recognise her now. Twelve years is a long time.

"Hey," Rachel said, reaching out to hold onto Danny's arm again, "can we go?"

"Sure," Danny nodded, taking her hand as he turned back to watch Dex disappear out of sight, "would you mind taking a detour on our way to your house? It's just that I need to check something out."

"Danny," Rachel sighed, looking him directly in the eye as she put two and two together, "this is not a good idea. You saw what he can do, do you really wanna piss him off after he told you to get lost?"

"Technically, he said he couldn't help," Danny said, shrugging a little as he took a step in the direction that Dex went, tugging gently at Rachel's hand to get her to go with him. "But you don't have to come. You can always go home if you want, I'm not going to stop you."

Rachel's face shifted from the nervous and fearful expression that she had been wearing all evening to disappointment. "I'm not going to let you chase after Pikachu on your own. You saved my life tonight, it's the least I can do."

Danny let out a wide smile and turned to follow Dex as he pulled Rachel along behind him. He was almost jumping with excitement as he walked down the path. They had to catch up quickly now that they couldn't see him, otherwise they would never know where he was going. Just because Dex could not help him didn't mean no one could, Danny hoped that there might be someone that Dex knew that could. That Lumin person the man had mentioned when Dex had arrived, maybe they could help him. If he was a teacher, or something like that, then maybe he knew more than Dex did. Maybe they could explain everything to him. Now that this thing had started, he could not let it get away from him. Danny could not watch Lilith be taken away from him. Not again.

CHAPTER FOUR
Definitely Not Stalking

Following Dex out of the park had been tricky, catching up to him had been the easy part as he had not gone that far but, staying out of his sight while keeping him in theirs was proving difficult. The stopping and starting was infuriating, like walking behind a slow walker on a narrow path with no way round. With every step, Danny became more excited and agitated. It made him feel as though he was stepping towards Lilith, he didn't want to wait, he wanted to run to her. But he couldn't risk getting caught and losing his chance. Rachel held tightly onto his hand as they ducked behind bushes and walls every so often to keep hidden.

"Danny," Rachel whispered as they hid behind a small wall that sat just before the foot of a mountain, "is this really a good idea? I mean, what if he knows we're here? What if he's luring us somewhere?"

"It'll be fine," Danny nodded, shuffling on his foot to get a better look at where Dex was heading, "he seems like one of the good guys anyway, I think he'll give us a chance."

"This isn't a comic book, Danny," Rachel hissed at him, not wanting to be there but not wanting to leave on her own either.

He gave her a weak smile before standing up to follow Dex again. Danny was not as sure as he said he was, Dex made him nervous, and he was certainly not prepared to protect himself, let alone Rachel as well, against him. Each step made his stomach turn, but he could not turn back now, it was not like he had anyone waiting for him, so he could take as long as he needed. However, he could not assume the same for Rachel.

Dex walked quite a way up the mountain before stopping next to a building with large gates and walls that was mostly hidden amongst the trees. Whatever kind of building it was, Danny couldn't tell because there was no way of seeing inside past the walls from where he was. They waited behind a tree as Dex knocked on a smaller door set into the gate. There were a few moments when they all held still and nothing happened, then the smaller door opened, and Dex walked inside. Danny stood up to take a closer look, but Rachel yanked hard enough on his arm to pull him back down.

"Stop," she said forcefully as Danny fell into the tree with a thump, "you've seen where he went, you can come back tomorrow. I'm sure your parents are worried about you, I'm certain my mom is going to kill me."

"I'll be fine," Danny said, chuckling slightly to himself and dusting off the dirt and bits of bark from his hoodie as he got back up, "but I'll take you home. I said 'detour' not vacation."

Danny walked Rachel back to his van. She had let go of his arm now that everything had calmed down, so he walked a little ahead of her as his stride was longer than hers was. He thought it would be better to give her a lift home rather than make her walk any further. She had been dragging her feet for the last twenty minutes and yawning every so often. The van was red and a little battered, but it was what he had, the passenger door was a little stiff, so he opened it for her.

"Thank you, for taking me home," Rachel said as Danny closed his door after getting in the van, "I know I forced you to take me with you then complained the whole time, so thank you. You didn't have to."

"It's no problem, really," Danny smiled as he turned the key in the ignition, "I've got nowhere else to be."

With a little frown at his comment, Rachel shifted in her seat to look at what was in the back. There was a soft seat that looked as though it folded out into a mattress, a bin bag sat next to it with sheets poking out of the top. The floor and the walls of the van were carpeted and had a few boxes stacked in the corner. Danny's rucksack hung off the back of Rachel's seat.

"Sorry it's not very Pinterest," Danny chuckled as he watched her staring at the back of the van, "but I got some fairy lights the other day, so I'm on my way."

As he watched the road, Danny reached behind his head and flicked a switch on a small box. The tiny lights that were littered around the roof of the van lit up like stars. He gave a little smile, he liked the lights, they certainly beat the torch he was using before. It was more calming, less like a spotlight.

"Danny?" Rachel asked, shuffling back as Danny drove down the road. She was a little nervous to ask, she was not sure if it were her place or whether she would come off as judgmental.

"Hm?"

"Do you live in this van?" she asked, holding her breath slightly as she watched his face.

"Yeah," Danny shrugged, finally pushing his hood down and wiping his wet hair away from his forehead. The front of his hair was darker because it was wet but behind it, the blonde could be seen better. The shaved sides were a lot darker than the rest of his head, showing that his hair was naturally a darker brown. "I lost my parents a while ago and trying to get a place is harder than it sounds, so van living."

Rachel did not live that far away from the park, so the drive was short. Danny pulled the van over to the curb outside her house and pulled the handbrake. Rachel gave him a small nod and a smile before hopping out of the van and walking to her front door. Wanting to make sure she got in okay, Danny didn't drive off immediately. As he waited, Rachel stopped just before she opened the front door.

"Danny, wait," she called, jogging back to the van door, "come in, you can sleep in the spare room, and I'll make some food. Come stay somewhere warm, it's raining, and you'll be cold in the van."

"The van's fine," Danny tried to tell her, to be polite, but a warm bed did sound tempting, "I put carpet on the walls."

He tapped happily against the side of the walls of the van.

"Daniel, was it?" an older woman appeared in the doorway, he assumed it was Rachel's mother, "are you a friend of my daughter's?"

"We actually just met tonight," Danny told her, trying not to be a pain, "I am a complete stranger."

"He saved me, I was almost attacked by some creepy guy in the park, but he stepped in," Rachel told her mother, "You're gonna need a plaster or something for that cut on your knee as well. He fought the guy off, Mom."

"Well, not completely," Danny stumbled over his words as he tried to play down the situation. He was not the best at receiving compliments or praise. "I tried but..."

"I made pasta bake if you want some, kid," Rachel's mother shrugged, stepping back to tell Rachel to go inside, "it's tomato and cheese."

Danny sat for a moment in a staring contest with Rachel's mother. He loved pasta more than anything, and he had not eaten since the morning. He got paid from his job tomorrow, but he had run out of food this morning. Giving in, Danny closed the window and jumped out of his door. Locking the van, he followed Rachel inside the house, letting her mother close the door behind them both.

CHAPTER FIVE
Lumin

Before even the sun could rise, Danny had got up, made the bed, and slipped down the stairs without waking anyone up. He didn't want to be a burden, this was not his house, and he didn't want to overstay his welcome. As he tiptoed across the carpet to reach the door, he let out a strangled screech as he tried to keep his voice down. Danny had been hit on the head with something hard at considerable speed. Turning, he looked down and saw an apple laying at his feet. With a quick glance up, he saw Rachel standing in the kitchen, facing away from him as she put bread in the toaster.

"What do you think you are?" she asked, not turning to look at him as she pushed down the lever on the toaster, "some kind of ninja?"

"I didn't want to bother you," Danny sighed, bending down to pick up the apple from the floor and walking over to her, "or your parents. You met me yesterday, I am grateful that you've been so kind to me, I am, but I can't just move in with you. I have to leave sooner or later."

"Danny, no-one was inviting you to move in. You can stay for breakfast," Rachel chuckled at his nervous expression, he clearly was not used to hospitality. She did not want to pry, but she couldn't help but wonder what his life had been like. He would tell her if he wanted to. "You should eat before going up to that creepy house in the mountains anyway."

Rachel slid a small plate across the counter at him and turned to open the cupboard, inviting Danny to decide what he wanted on his toast. He chose the jam and sat as he was instructed to. Danny had not had someone caring about his well-being for a long time, he was not used to being parented like this. It made him feel like a child again, but he found that he didn't mind so much, it allowed him to relax a little.

The trek back to the building with the big walls and gates was not difficult, it was the getting in bit that Danny had yet to think through. He stood with his backpack on, staring up at the tall gate, not sure what to do next. Knocking seemed obvious, but he was almost certain anyone inside would just tell him to leave immediately. He could not see a way to scale the walls, but he hadn't tried to yet. Then came the problem of what to do if he did get in. He would think of what to do when he got up there.

Danny gave a shrug and went up to one side of the gate, the large stones mere inches from his face. He reached up to feel just above the stone in front of him. Luckily for him, there was a groove in between the stones just big enough for him to rest his fingertips on. Finding a space for his foot, Danny began to climb. He had only reached a couple of feet before he was startled by his phone ringing, and he lost his balance. Danny hit the floor with a loud thud, he simply stared at the top of the wall for a moment while he listened to his ringtone. Before it went to voicemail, Danny reached into his pocket and looked at the display.

Rachel. He frowned for a moment and then answered it.

"How did you get my number?" He asked immediately, before she could even say hello, the phone pressed firmly against his ear as he lay in the fallen leaves.

"The only other number in your phone is your boss," Rachel said down the phone as Danny continued to lay on the floor, "that's sad."

"My life is sad, it adds to my aesthetic," Danny told her, still a little confused, "did you steal my phone while I was sleeping? How'd you get into it?"

"We don't need the details," Rachel said, brushing him off to get to her point. She leant on a counter in front of her as she stood away from the ice-cream bar in the place where she worked. "Anyway, how's it going? Did you get in?"

"You totally stole my phone," Danny sighed, not moving from his spot on the ground. He wasn't used to having friends, after leaving her house he hadn't expected to see or talk to Rachel again, so he was a little glad that she had broken into his phone.

"We're best friends now Danny, it's fine," Rachel jested, trying to lighten the mood, making sure to check that her boss wasn't watching her every so often.

"Considering you are my only friend, that sentence is pretty accurate," Danny mumbled as he sat up from the floor, huffing a little at his bad posture as he hunched his back.

"And now we're back to sad," Rachel sighed down the phone, sitting on the cabinet she had been leaning on as she waited for Danny to say something about how his mission was going.

"I tried to climb the wall, but it didn't work," Danny told her as he pushed himself out of a sitting position and got to his feet, "I think I'm gonna try again."

"Have you tried the door? Or knocking?" Rachel asked, sounding a little bored in her tone.

"Go give ice-cream to people that don't deserve it." Before Rachel could speak again in protest, Danny had hung up the phone on her.

Dusting off the dirt from the bits of him he could reach, Danny didn't notice that someone was watching him from the top of the wall. Danny put his hands back in place to climb, he placed his foot and looked up again. As soon as he did, he found himself in a staring contest with an older man with long, dark blonde hair and deep purple eyes. There were bags under the man's eyes which made him look like he had not slept in the past week. A pair of sunglasses sat gently between the fingers of the hand that lay over the edge of the wall.

"Can I help you?" the man asked, his tone dry and a little gruff as he frowned down at the teenager trying to climb his wall.

Stepping back from the wall, Danny stumbled a little before speaking. "Uh. Um. I met a kid yesterday, and he answered some questions, but he had to go, and he came here, so I was wondering if maybe I could ask a couple more."

"You're the kid that Dex met," the man said, shifting a little in his position to put his sunglasses back on, "are you an electricity wielder?"

Danny froze for a second, he wasn't exactly sure what a wielder was, but he knew that his answer would be important, it had been the same as when Dex had agreed to answer his questions, "Well, you see- "

"Can you produce electricity from your hands or not, kid?" the man asked, leaning a little further over the wall.

"Not exactly, no," Danny sighed, looking down at his feet. He could have lied, but there was no point. The ruse would have been up the second he stepped inside and was asked to prove it.

"Then I can't help you, I'm sorry," the man disappeared quickly back over the wall now that he had figured out whether he needed to talk to the teenager standing outside his property or not.

"Wait no! Please! This isn't about me!" Danny called out desperately as he jumped at the wall, "this is about my friend. Please, her name is Lilith, Lilith Romano."

"Romano!" the man exclaimed, darting rather quickly back to the edge of the wall, "why are looking for her?"

"She's my friend," Danny repeated, giving his best puppy dog eyes to try and gain some sympathy, but he gave up when the man was clearly unimpressed, and went with a determined frown instead. "Do you know her?"

"You should stop looking for her and live your own life, kid," the man said, calming down a little from his initial shock from hearing the name.

"Do you know her?" Danny pressed on; he was not going to give up now, not with a reaction like that. "Dex said you stick to your own, how do you know her? Is she okay?"

"When a six-year-old blows up a mile radius, taking out the majority of a town, you tend to hear about stuff like that," the man sighed leaning on the wall again as he talked to Danny, "or as I should say, a gas leak. But, given that you're here, I'm guessing you know that's not true."

"Gas leaks don't create giant monsters that smash houses like they're cardboard," Danny told him. That day was hard for him to remember, partly because he was so young but mostly because he lost everything that day, his home, his dog, his best friend. He didn't want to remember it.

"No, they don't," the man smiled as he watched Danny, the kid was smart, and he didn't rationalize away everything he had seen like most non-wielders do. It was a fresh change, "and they certainly don't leave little girls alive at the center of it, especially when everyone else dies. What makes you think she survived that?"

"I saw her," Danny said, his heart racing in his chest, he had never felt so close to an answer before. He just wanted to know that she was okay, to see that she was safe. "I wasn't in my house when it happened, me and my parents were out but she was still there when we got back. She was taken away by people like I saw yesterday."

"Well then, she's in good hands, and you should go home," the man said, suddenly changing his tune and trying to get Danny to leave again.

"I want to see her!" Danny shouted after the man as he disappeared out of sight again, he couldn't just give up now, not when he was closer to her than he had been in years, "tell me where she is!"

"I can't."

"Why not?"

"Because she's probably dead," the man finally snapped, reappearing again, "why can't you just be happy with being told an answer you'd want to hear. If you want probability, shadow wielding is dangerous and that kind of power cannot be contained inside the body for long, your friend is dead, or dying, so leave her in peace."

"Don't say that!" Danny shouted at him, slamming his hand against the wall as he did so. As his hand connected with the stone, he felt it burn and tense up like he had just hit a live wire. He screamed out in pain as he jumped back from the wall.

"What did you do to me?" Danny asked as he clutched his arm tight to his chest, stumbling back onto the floor.

"Oh, hang on a minute," the man sighed, pushing back from the wall, and disappearing again, "I'm coming down."

Danny grunted as he pulled his arm away from his chest to see lines where his skin had been burned. He only sat in the dirt for a few minutes before the door in the large gate opened and the man appeared.

"Let me see," he said as he walked over to him.

"No, what did you do to me?" Danny asked again, pulling his arm back from the man and shuffling away.

"Nothing, you did that to yourself, now let me see," the man said calmly, his voice was a lot gentler now as he crouched down next to Danny.

"What do you mean?" Danny asked, reluctantly handing over his burnt arm to the man.

"I watched you do it, remember, I saw it spark," the man said softly as he looked at the burn, "I'm Lumin, by the way, and you are?"

"Danny. Daniel. Daniel Andrews." Danny stumbled over his words as he tried to give the right information.

"Well, Danny, it seems like you can use electrical wielding," Lumin told him, "You're obviously just not very good at it."

"I can do it," Danny exclaimed excitedly, "all through the power of friendship."

"No," Lumin said, turning his arm over to look at it further, "you would have always been able to do this."

"Activated with the power of friendship," Danny continued, lifting his hand triumphantly as he spoke.

"Activated with the power of being very pissed off that I said your friend was dead," Lumin told him, "And look, you've got an older burn here too, you've done this before."

"You're no fun."

"You read too many comic books."

CHAPTER SIX
Lili

12 years earlier

It was late, Danny and Lilith had spent the whole day together, from school to them having dinner at the same table. It had been a while since he had been allowed to see her, Lilith's dad had kept her out of school for the past week because he said she had been sick, and Danny had not been allowed to go and see her. He had only wanted to take her something to make her feel better. Danny's mother, Kacey Andrews, had finally convinced Lilith's father to let Lilith come with them for Halloween this year because it was not in fact a day for the devil, but just one for kids to have fun. Lilith had been so excited but then the sickness came, and she was no longer allowed to go. That was what he had wanted to bring her, the sweets he had collected for her. However, now she had come back to school, Lilith's mother had agreed to let her stay with them for dinner after school so that they could spend a little more time together while her father was away on business for the next few days.

Sat at the table, Lilith's small arms lay under the tablecloth, tucked neatly in her lap. With the heating in the house on for the winter, she had taken her jumper off, revealing the bruises on her wrists and up her arms. Danny could not help but stare. He constantly had bruises all over him from playing outside, but these bruises were different. Lilith had not been outside in a long time.

"Lili," he whispered, leaning over to her in his seat, she turned without saying a word, "what happened to your arm? Did you fall down?"

Lilith did not speak, she simply paused for a second and then nodded. She had not been very talkative throughout the day; it worried the little boy to see his friend like that.

"Lili sweetie, can you pass these to Danny please," Mrs. Andrews said, handing Lilith a pot with vegetables in it.

"Yes ma'am," Lilith said politely, reaching up to take the pot, bruises on show for the whole table.

Danny watched as his parents gave each other a look, a look that generally was not his concern and he would not be told about it even if he asked. He was too young for that sort of thing, they would tell him, but now he was concerned because it involved his friend. If they were worried about her too, then he knew something was really wrong.

Dinner went on as normal, if a little tense, they laughed a little and Danny's mother asked Lilith a few questions but nothing too unusual which made it hard for Danny to figure out what was going on. It came to the end of the night and Lilith's mother came to pick her up, but Kacey wanted to talk first.

"Are you okay, Mary?" she asked in a hushed voice as Danny watched them from behind the kitchen door, "is everything okay at home? We are always here if you need us."

"Oh yes, everything is just fine," Mrs. Romano laughed off the question of concern as if it were one about shortbread, "Lili's having a little trouble controlling that little temper of hers, but that's nothing the Lord can't help with."

"Are you sure? She has bruises, is she hitting herself on things?" Kacey continued to question the wiry looking woman standing in front of her as Lilith hid just behind her mother's leg, "I don't want to make accusations, but it's worrying to see on a child."

Kacey had known Mary for a long time, from before either of them were married, she didn't want to believe that her friend would do something like that to a child, or even allow it.

"Oh, yes, those, those are..." Mrs. Romano trailed off a little as she looked down at Lilith who was pulling her sleeves over her hands, "yes, she'll thrash around you know, temper tantrums and the like. Father James thinks it's the grief with her brother and all. We're all struggling with Luke's death, but it seems to be a fight for this one."

"Of course, and if Father James is involved," Mrs. Andrews nodded, a little relieved that someone she trusted was involved, "Well, if everything is alright. She's been good as gold here, so if you ever want us to have her over again, she's more than welcome. If you need a night off or anything."

"Of course, thank you, Kacey," Mary smiled before taking Lilith's hand to walk her back to the car.

Danny edged his way out of the kitchen and down the hall to where his mother was standing to watch them go, but by the time he reached the door, it was shut.

"What are you up to, mister?" Kacey asked her son as he touched his hand to the door, trying to get as tall as he could on his toes, so he could see out the windows in the door.

"What's wrong with Lili?" he asked, looking up at her as she stepped away from the door.

"Nothing, baby, she's fine." She told him, just about making it to the living room door before stopping.

"No, she's not, I saw her arm, something's not okay," Danny said sternly, standing his ground, "you know it, I know you do."

"Everything is fine Danny, she's just struggling a bit with Luke's death," she tried to explain to him as gently as she could, "you remember when I told you that Luke went to live with Jesus, she misses him that's all."

"That doesn't make bruises," Danny argued, getting more and more frustrated with his mother as she avoided his questions, "that makes you cry."

"Not always Danny," his mother said, trying to keep her composure, but her voice was raising a little, "besides, Father James is involved, so she's in safe hands. She'll be okay, he won't let anyone hurt her."

"Father James doesn't know shit!" Danny yelled as he turned and sprinted up the stairs to his room.

"Daniel Andrews!" his mother shouted after him as the loud thuds of his feet running up the stairs echoed through the house.

He slammed the door to his bedroom as hard as he could, holding back the tears in his eyes with all he had. He could not bear to see Lilith hurt, and the fact it felt like no one was doing anything made him so angry that he did not know what to do. His frustration consumed him.

Kacey sighed, but she let him go. She didn't know what she would say to him, even if she did force her way into his room. Tell him to stop swearing when his friend was probably being abused? Even thinking that that made her skin crawl.

"Everything okay?" Jason Andrews asked his wife as she slid down the door frame of the living room door to sit on the floor.

"We have to do something Jase," she said, the pain of her helplessness clenching in her chest, making her want to just let the tears fall, "I want to trust Mary, but that man... who hits a child?"

"What do you want to do?" Jason asked, crouching down beside her, "because he'll fight you for them both. Now, if you want to get Mary to pack up and run, we can probably make that work but, I won't risk Danny's life for them - I know it sounds bad, but he's my son. Lilith isn't my daughter and-"

"I know," Kacey's bottom lip quivered as she turned her head to look up at the ceiling, "Aurora's still out there somewhere, and she wouldn't just let him go if she found us."

Laying a hand gently onto his wife's shoulder, Jason moved to sit next to her as she finally gave in and started to cry into her knees.

"Fuck her," she sobbed, leaning into Jason's arms.

CHAPTER SEVEN
Hit The Tree

Present

The atmosphere in the room was awkward. No one had spoken since Lumin had helped Danny up from the ground. Now though, Danny sat with his knees tightly together and his hands tucked into his lap as he waited for Lumin to turn back and explain what was going to happen next. The tired looking man, with dark blonde hair which was pulled back into a bun on the top of his head, had brought him inside the walls and led him to a building just across a courtyard on the estate. Currently, he seemed to be digging around in a cupboard looking for something.

"Give me your arm again," Lumin finally spoke as he found whatever he was looking for, turning, and walking back towards where Danny was sitting.

Handing his arm over, Danny watched as Lumin lay a cool gauze over his burnt skin, the moisture instantly soothed the pain that came with it. He watched Danny's face as he wrapped the bandage around his hand and arm.

"How's that?" Lumin asked softly as he secured the bandage on his arm, "not too tight?"

"No, thank you, it's great," Danny said with a smile as he tapped gently on the bandaged part of his arm, "what happens now? Are you going to help me?"

"I have no choice," Lumin sighed, taking a seat in the chair across from Danny, "if you try and use your wielding again, and I suspect that you will, you could seriously hurt yourself. Having the electricity in your body amplified, if not controlled properly, can cause anything from superficial burns and muscle twitches to heart attacks and seizures, so you stay. At least until I'm happy you're going to be safe."

"Training montage, go!" Danny yelled as he punched with all his strength against the tree in front of him, "ow."

"Are you even trying?" Lumin asked, sighing as he folded his arms, having watched Danny fail to produce electricity for the last fifty minutes.

"I am trying," Danny complained as he geared up for what felt like his hundredth hit against the tree.

His knuckles were sore and starting to bleed at this point. Danny scowled as he placed his feet exactly where Lumin had instructed at the beginning. With a deep intake of breath, Danny drew back his right fist in line with his shoulder. In time with his exhale, Danny hit out and struck the tree. Ripping more into his skin, he felt the electricity travel down his shoulder, through his arm, and out of his fist. The wood of the tree burned as it connected with Danny's fist. In his surprise, Danny took a sharp inhale which brought the electricity back to him, hitting him in the hand, and singeing his knuckles a little.

"Careful," Lumin laughed, jumping a little at the sudden success, "control your breathing, it'll help control your thinking. Then it won't hurt as much."

Danny rubbed his thumb across his knuckles and smiled when he saw that the burn was significantly less than before. Progress was progress, even if he was still getting hurt.

In an effort to show him some encouragement, Lumin gave Danny a firm pat on the shoulder and a brief smile, but before he could say anything. a small voice distracted him from their training session.

"Min-min!" it called, causing Lumin to snap his head round in the direction it had come from. A little girl, she couldn't be older than three, was running across the field, laughing maniacally, as a woman came chasing after her.

"Clara!" the woman shouted, slowing down a little as she saw Lumin standing watching the little girl, "Lumin is busy, come on."

"Oh, it's alright, we can take a break," Lumin smiled, crouching down so that he was closer to Clara's height, "gives you a chance to meet our newest student, Danny, Amelia. Amelia, Danny."

Lumin then didn't speak to either of them, he just sat on the floor and let Clara babble at him and tug at the loose strands of his hair, smiling like a proud uncle as he watched her. His mood had significantly improved the moment he had seen her.

There was a brief silence as Amelia and Danny stared at each other, then Amelia started the conversation, "so... electrical wielding. Cool, right?"

"Yeah, well, kinda hot actually," Danny joked, waving his burnt hand a little as he spoke.

Amelia laughed as she looked at the burn marks across his knuckles and the scorched bandage that was hanging loosely around his arm. "I have gloves that can help with that, for practice. They're insulating. They're made from this special material... if you're interested," Amelia told him, rocking a little on her heels. She looked nervous to tell him, like she wasn't sure how he would take it.

"They make those?" Danny asked excitedly, stretching out his fingers to try and imagine the gloves on his hands. The idea of a whole new world of technology was almost overwhelming.

"I did," Amelia said, a little sheepish, as if she was testing the waters of how much Danny actually cared.

"Woah! You must be really smart," Danny smiled, looking at Amelia with wide eyes, "what are they made of? Is it like rubber and stuff, those are insulators, right?"

"Yes, yes they are," Amelia almost squealed with excitement. While Dex and Lumin were happy to listen if she wanted to talk about her projects, they had never shown the same enthusiasm as Danny, although they did want to know what she was up to. "I made my own synthetic blend of a rubber-based material, similar to the compound found in electrical wielders muscle tissue that protects us from deep tissue burns. And that protects the hand from call back shocks like the ones on your knuckles. And on the knuckles of the gloves, there are copper plates so if you're fast enough, you can use them as a taser from the built-up charge."

Danny stared at Amelia for a moment, not fully understanding what she had just told him. He had never been the best at science, so he couldn't wrap his head around how it all could work, but it certainly sounded very interesting.

"That's so cool," Danny smiled, after giving up on trying to work out what it all meant and just trusting that Amelia knew what she was talking about.

"I make a lot of things, if you ever wanted to check them out, I'd be happy to show you!" Amelia beamed widely, her cheeks flushed a little red from the excitement of being able to talk about her projects with someone, "I make all sorts of gear, it comes in really handy especially when you're basically a human battery."

"That'd be cool, yeah, thank you," Danny told her, mirroring her movement as she held her arms tight to her body with her fists jumping up and down in front of her in excitement.

CHAPTER EIGHT
Danny VS Dex

Days later, Lumin had an idea. Comfortable now in Danny's ability to produce electricity without hurting himself, after putting the teenager through several more hours of breathing exercises and training steps, he now wanted to see how Danny coped taking a punch. He knew Danny would never get a finger on Dex, but he decided to present it as a spar anyway.

"I just wanna let her know I'm doing okay," Danny said, holding his phone tightly in his hands in front of Lumin, "she helped me a lot, I can't just ditch her like she never existed, that's not fair."

"Alright, but you can't tell this Rachel girl anything about the wielding," Lumin told him firmly, folding his arms across his chest, "non-wielders can get spooked, they don't see us because they don't want to. It's just safer for everyone."

"Oh yeah, of course," Danny smiled, dialing her number immediately and walking away from Lumin, "I completely understand."

"So, he's doing good then? He's getting the hang of the whole wielding thing?" Rachel asked as she stood next to Lumin watching Danny and Dex prepare for their spar. Danny couldn't contain his excitement the second she had answered the phone and had told her everything that he knew, she had come to join him as soon as her shift at the ice cream bar had finished. Rachel looked up at Lumin while she stood in her pale blue uniform, the hat clutched in her hand.

"Yeah, he's starting to get it," Lumin told her, frowning at Danny as he happily waited for the beating he was about to receive, "he's not the best wielder I've seen. He's definitely a late bloomer."

Rachel nodded as Danny drew back his foot, ready to fight. "Late bloomer? So are wielders born then, it's just something that happens?"

"Hmm, yeah, wielding is a genetic ability," Lumin told her, watching the two boys closely, "He would have probably had a parent or close relative that maybe didn't talk about it, so he never learned. Most wielders do it by accident when they're children though, so this is a little unusual."

Lumin glanced over at Rachel and then backed up to see that the two boys were ready. Even at fourteen, Dex was one of his strongest students. Danny had no chance at winning this match, but that wasn't the point. The point of this training session was to show him what it felt like to be hit with electricity and how to control it once it had hit his skin. It also gave him a chance to practice how to pull his punches so that he wouldn't hurt anyone he didn't want to.

"Anybody dies, I'm gonna be pissed," Lumin called over to them, his arms crossed as he stood back with the others, "begin."

Dex did exactly as he was trained and did not waste a second. His first step forward was visible, but then he became a blur. Danny's eyes widened; he couldn't do anything. Dex hit him square in the stomach, sending Danny flying. Landing him on his back behind Dex.

"Ow," Danny groaned, clutching at his stomach with one hand, the other outstretched on the grass.

"Where does it hurt?" Lumin asked, making sure everything was alright to continue.

"Yes."

"Okay, get up."

Pushing through the pain, Danny got back to his feet and pulled his hands up to his face, making sure to hunch down a little this time to protect his abdomen as well. He wanted to at least land something, prove that he was capable, so the next time Dex took a dash at him, Danny hit out. Sending any kind of electricity he could manage, out in a punch. A swing and a miss. Dex dipped out of the way with ease and hit Danny again, making him land face first this time.

Instead of complaining, Danny just pushed himself back up. He was sure he could do something this time. He was getting closer, and he could feel it. If he just kept trying. He shook out the aches left in his body, making sparks fall off from his hands. Lifting his arms back up, ready to take another hit. Danny kept his focus. Nothing would distract him. He shouldn't act too fast, only when he needed to. Trust your instincts, trust your gut, he told himself.

Dex had decided to give him a chance, he wanted to know if he could land a shot on him after the last one. He had actually had to dodge him, rather than Danny hitting out blindly. But he couldn't be sure if it was just a coincidence. At this point, Dex was getting tired, so a shorter dash was welcome. Stopping himself just before where Danny was standing, Dex charged up his fist, ducking out of the way of Danny's punch; he could feel the electricity touch on the tip of his ear as it passed his head. This boy was definitely capable of landing a shot on him. And if he wasn't careful, it would be sooner than expected. Danny had reacted quickly and was already taking another swing at him. Dex hit out with the power he had created and punched up, catching Danny in the chest.

Hitting the ground with a thud, Danny landed on his back.

"Ahh," he screamed as he clutched at his chest, "am I gonna have a heart attack? Am I having a heart attack?"

"What?" Rachel exclaimed, running over to him, a step behind Lumin who had also rushed over once he had screamed out.

"No, calm down," Lumin told him once he was happy that Danny was not in fact having a heart attack.

"But you said, you said that extra electricity in the body can give me a heart attack," Danny panted as he sat himself up, "I got hit in the chest, that's where my heart is. Is it worse? Am I having a stroke?"

"God, I hope so," Lumin sighed as he grabbed Danny by the arm and pulled him back to his feet, "you're fine, Dex wouldn't hurt you. Let's take a break for now, dust yourself off."

"Okay," Danny nodded, as he tried to recompose himself after his brief freak out, "you're right."

CHAPTER NINE
A Fountain Conversation

Feeling a little disappointed with himself, Danny sat on the edge of the fountain in the courtyard, his head drooped down as he looked at the floor. He had hoped that he would have done better in the spar against Dex. After practicing for two days straight, the progress that he had been making had boosted his confidence so much that losing to Dex really knocked him, especially after not being able to land a single hit on him.

As usual, his thoughts drifted to her. Lilith's face. That night, he had only just been able to see her when he reached the rubble where his town used to be. She had been paler than usual and her hair completely different, but it was her eyes that he remembered most. Like a snapshot projected into his mind. They had been pure white for the first second that they had made eye contact, and then faded back to the dark blue that they usually were. The image that kept him going with unrelenting fury, but also crippled him every time he remembered.

As Danny sat, Amelia, the student that he had met earlier, came to join him at the fountain.

"You okay?" she asked, leaning forward to try and look at his face to see how he was feeling. The most she got was a side profile with hidden eyes as the blonde part of his hair fell limp over his face.

"Yeah," Danny sighed, sitting back up and turning to look at Amelia. She still looked the same from earlier, her hair tied back into a ponytail with a bandana badly holding her fringe out of her eyes.

"Don't be too hard on yourself," Amelia told him as she watched the sullen expression of the once excitable boy, "Dex never lets anyone win, he's grumpy like that. His dad was a pretty big deal amongst the wielding community, especially with electricity wielders. So, he feels the need to be the best because his dad was so proud of him when he was training with him."

"Why'd he stop?" Danny asked, frowning a little, "why is he training with Lumin now?"

"His dad died," Amelia explained, Dex was relatively calm about the whole ordeal. He would talk about it if asked, so Amelia didn't feel like he would mind if she let Danny know, "not everyone thinks that wielding is this amazing ability that people have, some people get scared and lash out. And we live in America, where the worst-case scenario is easily accessible."

"Oh," Danny froze, not knowing what to say. He hadn't realised that that was something he would have to worry about now. The guilt for bringing Rachel in without talking it through with them first suddenly hit him. He hadn't known her that long, and even though he didn't think that she would be the type of person to do something like that, but he couldn't have been sure, and neither could they. Danny had been lucky. If he had been wrong about her, then he would have learned this the hard way instead. He shook himself, "So, why do you train here?"

"Me?" Amelia smiled, a little surprised that he would ask about her when they had been talking about him and Dex, "Lumin's a great teacher, and he gave me my own lab to work on my inventions, so I love it here. My daughter, Clara, is cared for by all of us, I have a place to stay for free, and I have people around me who really get who I am. I wouldn't wanna be anywhere else."

A small smile sat on Danny's face as he looked over at Amelia. She made him feel so much more comfortable with the whole situation, her welcoming nature really helped him feel better about everything going on around him.

"What about you?" Amelia asked him, nudging him in the shoulder as she spoke, "what do you want to train for?"

"My friend, or my—I don't know," Danny stumbled over what he wanted to say, he knew how he felt, but how it really was, was likely a different story. "She was my best friend when we were little, but I haven't seen her in twelve years. I don't know what she is to me now, if she were here, I'd still be there for her, but I can't know for sure about her. I should have been there for her before, but I wasn't."

"You're losing me a little," Amelia laughed nervously as Danny spiraled into his own thoughts, "who's your girlfriend?"

"The girl with me? She's not my girlfriend. I'm talking about Lilith. She was my best friend from, like, birth to first grade," Danny explained, "but then, when we were six, something happened. She destroyed my whole town, my house was gone, all the neighbours. People died that day, and I can't get angry at her. The only images I have in my mind are her laughing in a park and her being taken away from me by men in black suits. Her hair was completely black, I barely recognised her, it used to be so blonde, almost white."

Amelia smiled as she reached up to brush at the longer part of his hair on the top of his head, "like this blonde?"

"I tried," Danny laughed, pulling his hair down over his eyes to where he could see it, "I've only got me, so I could never get my hair that light without burning it off. Mine's too dark for that."

"It's cute that you remember her like that, you're a good friend, Danny," Amelia chuckled, standing up to leave him in peace now that she knew he was okay. She had work to do and so did he, she would talk more with him later.

CHAPTER TEN
Anomalies

The room that Amelia had taken Danny to was dark, he wasn't sure if that was on purpose or whether it simply had no light. A large chalkboard stood in front of him with a white sheet pulled down over it. He sat in a desk type chair in the center of the room, wanting to wait patiently, but Amelia had dragged him into the dark room with very little explanation as to what she was going to do, so he couldn't help but fidget.

"You ready?" she chirped from behind him.

Danny looked back when there was a sudden glow of light behind him, Amelia's face was lit up menacingly with the electricity that bounced between her hands.

"Uhm…" Danny stuttered, leaning away from her as far as his chair would let him. He had been beaten up too much to not want to duck if she was going to attack him again in another crazy exercise.

With a smile, Amelia pumped the electricity in her hands into an old projector; it flickered on and shone a screen onto the white sheet on the black board. Danny turned back round to see that the projection showed a very basic looking PowerPoint that said 'Anomalies' in comic sans.

"What's an anomaly?" Danny asked, frowning as he watched Amelia walk up to the front of the room.

"I'll tell you," Amelia sighed, picking up the remote from the table. She clicked it aggressively to go to the next slide. "Anomalies are any residual energy left over from acts of wielding. All wielders can create anomalies, most are created by accident. Electrical anomalies can form in a wide range of ways, from static shocks to semi-living balls of lightning, depending on the amount of energy left over and the complexity of the wielding move."

"So, I have to be careful about making them," Danny nodded, staring at the stock photo of an electric shock and the grainy image of the ball of lightning, "because I'm an idiot."

"No," Amelia said sternly, a strong look of concentration on her face as she made sure he understood that she didn't think that he was stupid, "because you don't know what you're doing right now. I can tell you've already created small ones because of the burns on your hands. If the energy isn't used up, it's residual. And residual energy is an anomaly."

"You will need to learn how to deal with more complex anomalies if you chose to continue down this path with us," Lumin's voice made Danny jump a mile, he had not heard him enter the room and hearing it suddenly right next to him was something he wasn't expecting. "But because you are still learning, we will deal with the more complex one's for you. They can be very dangerous, so to keep you safe, you won't have to handle them at all, or at least on your own, until I trust you're ready."

Lumin made his way over to where Amelia was standing and tugged at the bottom of the white sheet to make it retract so that he could use the blackboard. As he reached for the chalk, the projector flickered off, causing Danny to turn and see that Dex had turned it off. The younger boy walked up the room and took a seat next to Danny.

"Where's Rachel?" Dex asked. He seemed different from his usual stoic resolve, almost nervous to ask.

"She had to go to work," Danny told him, trying to get a read on why he cared, but it wasn't really his business, so he decided not to press him about it. He received a nod from Dex then they both turned back to Lumin.

"You see, anomalies are created through a great output of wielding energy, varying of course between wielding types," Lumin explained, drawing an L shape on the blackboard, "wielding types like shadow and electricity require greater outputs of energy and therefore anomalies are more common. To combat this, we must raise the skill level of the wielder through training."

As he spoke, Lumin drew a line from the join in the L shape, showing that it was a graph. Along the y axis, he wrote skill. Along the x, he wrote power. Shading in under the line he drew, he pointed an arrow to the shaded area.

"This is how anomalies are formed." He pointed to the shaded area on the graph that showed where power overtook skill. "Skill is arguably much more important than power, even the weakest of wielders can have the strongest attacks if they have complete control."

"So, I can be just as strong as you guys one day," Danny beamed, his eyes sparkling with excitement, "even though I'm not that powerful, if I practice, I can be strong too."

"You're progressing quite quickly," Lumin told him, perching himself on a cabinet next to him, "you're probably more powerful than you think. We'll have to keep the training up as you progress. The more energy you put out, the worse the anomaly could be."

"But I can still help people," Danny's voice softened as he looked up at Lumin, all he wanted was to use his wielding to help people. If he couldn't do that, then he didn't know why he had this gift.

"We're not superheroes," Lumin told him gently, "We can do our best, but we're still just people. You're not immortal, and your body will break. It's your choice how you use your wielding, just know your limits."

Danny gave him a firm nod to show that he understood. Since even before his parents died, he had been working hard to become stronger, to protect the kids around him. He had gotten in a lot of trouble at school for stepping in when he saw his classmates being bullied. So what if there had been a fight, at least it was fair when he stepped in. He wanted to be ready if anyone tried to hurt Lilith again. When he found her, and he had never thought that he wouldn't, he wanted to be able to protect her the way he never could when they were six.

CHAPTER ELEVEN
Side Effects

Danny didn't stop. For the next week all he did was train, focusing on channelling the electricity in his body and steadying his mind as much as he could, so he could gain better control. Lumin had been right, the more he practiced, the more he could feel the power inside him building. It scared him, but he knew he had to push past that fear, even though Lumin said that he should still be mindful of it. He didn't want to hurt himself or someone else by pushing himself too fast.

"Hit me again," Danny called out, an electrical burn stinging his face as he smiled through the pain of it.

"Enough," Dex grunted, waving him off after spending the afternoon beating Danny up. He was tired and his shoulder hurt after Danny had skimmed it with his fist, giving him a muscle cramp. "I'm done."

Danny stood back up properly and stretched. He supposed he could go and hit the tree again, he still felt tingly from the energy still coursing through his muscles Jumping a little on the spot to use up the energy, he turned when he heard Lumin calling his name.

"You're in luck Daniel," Lumin said, throwing a packet of almonds at Dex who looked grateful for the snack, Danny simply grimaced a little at the sound of his full name, "there's an anomaly at the edge of the city. It's your first mission to watch it get dismantled. Dex and Amelia will be going with you, they'll be taking care of it, but you'll learn a lot by watching them."

Danny gave a double thumbs up as Dex tipped the full packet of almonds into his mouth, his cheeks bulging as he struggled to chew them. Happy that everyone was informed, Lumin passed a water bottle to Dex.

"Make sure to sleep in the car," he told him as he turned while Dex began to try and guzzle the water with his mouth full, "Amelia will have your back, but you don't want to be off your guard."

Dex gave a nod as he tried not to choke. He swallowed hard to get rid of the almonds and coughed slightly.

"Do I not get a snack?" Danny asked, dancing on his toes as he made his way over to Dex who was still drinking his water.

"How are you feeling?" he asked, screwing the cap back onto the empty bottle.

"Tingly," Danny replied, wiggling his fingers in front of his face as he smiled manically while fidgeting, like his whole body was full of electricity.

"You'll be fine," Dex yawned, turning to walk in the direction that Lumin had gone in, "you're buzzed, it can be a side effect. Other side effects include very not buzzed."

Danny leaned forward in his seat, pulling his seat belt as far as it would go, while Dex slept in the front passenger seat. He wanted to be able to talk to Amelia while he looked out of all the windows, but she was driving. He was excited to see what kind of anomaly they would be facing. They had shown him countless pictures over the past few days, but he was excited to see one up close.

"Be careful," Amelia told him, glancing away from the road only for a second to see where he was and then back to watch where she was driving.

"Sorry," he said, sitting back into his seat properly, "I'm just excited. I put the suit on, and it's like...BAM...ya know. Superhero suit up kind of thing."

Danny tugged slightly at the rubbery material of his new suit, Amelia had made it long sleeved now that they were well into the Autumn and the suit would likely be the only thing that wouldn't burn off of his body when he used his wielding.

"You'll get your chance," Amelia chuckled, reaching over, and pushing Dex in the shoulder until he began to stir, "we're almost there."

Dex sort of grunted at her as he rubbed his eyes, squinting at the sunlight and stretching as Amelia pulled the car over.

"Superhero time," Amelia chimed, turning back to smile at Danny, who beamed back at her. She only received an eye roll from Dex.

CHAPTER TWELVE
Shadow Wielder

They had arrived in a kind of junkyard. It was such a large expanse of space that no one would see them wielding, which was lucky for Danny's first mission because if he messed up it wouldn't matter too much. The three of them stood together, having spotted the floating ball of what looked like electrical wiring. They needed to explain the plan of attack so that Danny could learn about how everything worked.

"I'll dismantle it," Amelia told them, "To dismantle an anomaly like this you basically just stick your hand in it. Grab onto one of the wires and channel all the energy through you to dissipate it. Dex will be watching my back in case one of the wires decides to go rogue."

"Great, great plan, straight forward," Danny nodded, a frown of concentration on his face as he looked up to where the anomaly was, "new question, who's she? And what's she doing?"

The other two wielders looked up to see a young woman with jet black hair, half of it pulled back into a bun, walking slowly towards the anomaly. She had a black and white, long sleeve top on with a kind of protective vest over the top, which made Dex frown.

"Hey!" Amelia called, stepping forward and waving her hand towards the woman to try and get her attention, "you need to step back from there! It's not safe!"

The woman stopped and half turned towards them. An emblem was revealed on her chest that caused a panic in both Dex and Amelia, a black circle with white outline and a white semicircle inside. But Danny wasn't looking at the emblem, he was too captivated by her eyes. They were tired and darker than he remembered, but they were hers, there was no mistaking them. It was like he could feel it in his chest. There she was. Lilith. Alive.

"Lili," he mumbled as Dex and Amelia both shot their arms across his chest to protect him and stop him from running forward, "Lili!" he cried.

Lilith Romano frowned slightly before turning back to the anomaly.

"Danny stop," Dex yelled at him, moving in front of him and grabbing him by the shoulders as he tried to dodge past the two of them, "you want to play superheroes? That's the villain. You need to go back to the car. Now."

As he tried to reason with him, Lilith had brought her hands together and made the shape needed to form a dog when doing shadow puppets. She held it for a moment before tilting it down slightly; a giant shadow wolf launched out from behind her, billowing black smoke in its wake. The three electrical wielders ducked and huddled together as the monstrous creature roared and leaped onto the anomaly, devouring it in its jaws. Lilith could barely be seen amongst the clouds of smoke.

The haze of smoke in front of her eyes blurred the three people standing several feet from her, Lilith tilted her head as she watched them argue, they were too far for her to hear them. They could be the students that Emrick wanted her to show herself to, but they could also just be non-wielders in the wrong place. If they did nothing, she would kill them, but she decided to wait for a moment before attacking.

The girl stepped forward and lit up her hand with sparks, a deep frown on her face as she watched Lilith through the smoke. She looked past the girl to the boy with the dark hair on the sides of his head, the top obviously dyed. He looked familiar, and she wondered if it could be him. Lilith shook the thought from her head. What would he be doing here? Danny had no reason to know about the wielding world. It was probably someone else.

"Get him back to the car," Amelia ordered, as she kept her eyes on the smoke that was thinning, revealing the young woman watching them from where she stood, "I'll be right behind you. If Emrick's making moves, we need Lumin. We need to get out of here now."

"She's not dangerous," Danny argued as Dex began to push him back towards the car, his feet dragging along the floor, "she's probably just scared, please let me go talk to her. Let me see her, please."

"She is more powerful than any of us," Dex pleaded with him, pushing against Danny with everything he had, "if she decided to kill us, we couldn't stop her. Just look at that thing, she made it without a sweat, what else do you think she can do?"

"She won't hurt us," Danny's voice was softening as he saw the broken look in her eyes. Her body was strong, but she looked exhausted, the light that he loved so much was gone. "Please. She's my friend," he whispered softly.

"Not here," Dex told him, grabbing him by the hair, and forcing Danny to look at him, "we need Lumin if we want to stand a chance." Reluctantly, Danny stopped fighting against Dex and turned to run with him back to the car, Amelia followed close behind. When he imagined seeing her again, this had not crossed his mind. He couldn't protect her if he was fighting her. Everything felt wrong as they drove away from the wolf that was slowly dispersing into the air, he couldn't hold in his tears as he curled up in the back seat.

Arc One:
PART TWO

CHAPTER THIRTEEN
Old Memories

Lumin sat with his head in his hands, his heart hammering wildly as he ran through every thought and memory. A woman with earthy brown eyes knelt in front of him, looking up as she tried to ease his hands from his face, so she could talk to him properly.

"Hey," she said softly, tilting her head to try and gain eye contact with him, "Emrick wasn't going to hide forever. He had big plans, and if he's showing himself again, he's probably ready to get started with them."

"She's alive," Lumin whispered, more to himself than to her, "she can't be. Power like that, that out of control. She should be dead."

"Who?" she asked, frowning at him as he lifted his head, "who's still alive?"

"Lilith Romano," Lumin's voice was quiet, making absolutely sure that Fern was the only person that heard him.

"But that's-" Fern started but she didn't seem to want to finish her sentence, completely taken aback by his statement.

"Yeah."

"Lili," Fern mumbled, reeling from the familiarity of the surname, "You don't think Aurora still- she was looking for a Romano, wasn't she? Maybe they got away."

"Yes, she was," Lumin cut her off in his dazed state, he felt like he was floating through the conversation, "but I don't want to think about Lilith Romano still in the hands of that woman. We know Lilith is still with Emrick. That's as far as we need to take it. He's our problem."

"Okay," her voice soft as she looked at the fear in his eyes. They had good reason to be afraid. Shadow wielders tended to be very angry people, and when angry people are handed the power of a god it is inevitably going to get dangerous.

The door creaked as it opened, and three heads popped through and began inspecting the large plants that blocked Fern and Lumin from their line of sight.

"So, plant wielders can turn into plants," Danny hummed as he stroked his chin in concentration as he examined one of the large leaves closely, "what an interesting ability. I wonder if we can become pure electricity."

"Can a plant wielder really do that?" Dex asked, glancing up at Amelia, who seemed just as interested in the leaf as Danny was.

"Not as far as I know," Amelia muttered as she lifted the leaf gently with the tips of her fingers, "it would be an interesting theory to look at since shadow wielders can become shadow, or mist as they call it."

"We can't," Fern said, making the three of them jump and push past the leaves to see her and Lumin sitting on a sofa that had two spiky looking succulents at either side of it.

"Oh, hi Fern," Amelia smiled, stepping into the room so that Danny and Dex could get past her, "Clara and I have been watering your plants for you while you were away. Clara loved helping with them so much, she can't wait to meet you properly."

"Thank you." Fern smiled sympathetically as the two boys stepped awkwardly into view.

"And never try to turn yourself into pure electricity," Lumin told them firmly, steadying his breathing and putting on his best teacher voice, "You'll die. People have tried, the body can't handle that much electricity."

"That's a shame," Danny sighed, scuffing his feet a little, "would've been so cool, like shoo shoo - gone - back again - I mean Dex kinda does that now but that's like another level. But what are we going to do to save Lilith, because these two have been telling me how bad this Emrick guy is, she must be terrified."

"Danny," Lumin said gently, knowing that this was going to be hard for him to hear, "Lilith was wearing his emblem, she was out on her own. Emrick isn't holding her captive. She works for him."

"Then he's clearly lied to her," Danny snapped as he watched Lumin give him the same face that his mother used to use when he would ask about Lilith, and she didn't know how to get it through to him that she was dead. But his mother had been wrong, there was no reason why Lumin wouldn't be wrong now. "Lilith isn't evil."

"You haven't seen her since she was six," Lumin said more firmly, trying to get Danny to understand that they would likely have to fight her, "she's not a little kid anymore, she's had a long time for that anger to fester. And with Emrick behind her, he'd only fuel it, letting her lash out as violently as she wants."

"You don't even know her," Danny argued, glaring down at Lumin, "she doesn't want to hurt people. All she did was get rid of the anomaly, which is what we were there to do."

"We already know that she's a murderer," Lumin told him, standing up so he was level with Danny.

"That wasn't her fault," Danny's chest felt tight as he held his ground, "she didn't mean to."

"She still did it," Lumin's frown deepened, and his voice was firm, "she's capable of killing hundreds of people within minutes. She's his nuclear bomb. Are you going to be able to talk down the girl you don't even know any more if Emrick decides to detonate her?"

Danny had nothing to say. He held silent as he stared up at Lumin, not knowing if she would listen to him if he spoke to her. Come to think of it, he didn't even know if she would recognise him. He had recognised her straight away; he would be crushed if she had forgotten him.

CHAPTER FOURTEEN
Lilith

A black wolf walked amongst the foliage, leaving wisps of black smoke as it went, its pure white eyes glancing back at its maker as she sat watching. Wrapped in a blanket, Lilith had chosen to spend her morning outside, on a bench in the garden, just spending time in the open air with her dog. The beast tread carefully though it had no need to, it was barely solid.

As her eyelids hung heavy over her eyes, a man with neatly combed black hair and a white shirt with sleeves rolled up to his elbows walked towards her. He had a soft, sort of kind expression as he sat on the bench next to her, pushing the edge of her blanket out of his way.

"Lilith, you shouldn't be wasting your energy like that," Emrick told her, leaning back as he watched her more than the misty dog that wandered around in front of them. "We've got a lot of work to do"

"It barely takes anything," Lilith muttered, not taking her eyes from the wolf.

"Still, I don't want you risking hurting yourself for mild entertainment," Emrick sighed. He had taken care of her since she was ten years old. Watching her push her limits for years and seeing her use her wielding so casually made him proud to see the strength and control he had taught her. "Where's Astor anyway? Isn't he usually following you around?"

"He's probably still asleep," Lilith told him, finally removing her eyes from her wolf, and dispersing it into the air with a wave of her hand, "he's not an early bird."

"Lazy, is what he is," Emrick commented, rolling his eyes as he readjusted himself in his seat, "he needs to be more productive, harder working."

"Astor works hard," Lilith laughed, sitting up with her legs crossed and placing two closed fists onto her ankles, she formed a small gorilla that began to hop around the bench, "he just doesn't like to be awake. We've all been there."

The gorilla jumped and clung to the back of the bench, reaching up and grabbing Emrick by the jaw. He laughed slightly as the monkey climbed over his shoulder and into his lap, patting its feet a little before reaching up again and putting its arms around his neck to hug him. Emrick sighed and hugged the shadow gorilla back, glancing over at Lilith's hand which was delicately in a puppeteer position, she hadn't let it go yet, she was still controlling it.

"Disperse the gorilla, Lilith," he told her, letting go and turning to her as she relaxed her hand, letting the smoke that formed the gorilla float into the air, thinning until it disappeared. "Come on, we've got Christians to kill if we want to rid the world of their wickedness."

Lilith laughed at his joking tone as he mimicked the way Christians used to speak to them, like they were some kind of sinful demon for just existing with the power they were born with, an accident of birth.

"And wake up Astor," Emrick told her as he stood from the bench, reaching out and taking her by the chin so that she was looking at him, "you may have fallen, Lilith, but you're still an angel. You're going to save us all."

"You really think so?" Lilith smiled tiredly as she looked up at him.

"I know it." Emrick smiled down at her as he let go of her face and started to walk back inside, "now that you've spooked Lumin we're probably going to see him next time we go out, three on one is hardly fair. Astor needs to be awake and training."

"Four," Lilith corrected him, making him turn back to look at her, "there were three of them at the junkyard."

"Did you get a good look at the newcomer?" he asked, frowning a little as he thought about who she might have seen that wouldn't have tried to fight her. Lilith just shook her head. "Okay, hopefully they're just some untrained kid. You'll be able to take them out easily, but still take Astor with you. He'll be able to help."

Lilith nodded as he turned and went back inside the house. She was ready for a good fight, and Lumin was meant to be very strong, his students too. But everyone she met told her she was the most powerful shadow wielder they had seen since Aurora. She could take them; Astor could burn the churches while she dealt with Lumin and his wannabe superheroes.

CHAPTER FIFTEEN
The Incident

12 years ago

The room was dark, like it usually was. The light in the hallway was on and illuminated Lilith's doorway enough for her to see the silhouette of her father standing over her. He was probably glaring like usual. Sometimes an air of disappointment or pity could be seen through his rage. But now she could hardly see his face in the shadows.

"Why has God forsaken this family with this child?" he asked, looking at the six-year-old sitting in front of him, "you were supposed to be a saviour for us, a miracle. But the devil has taken you from us. This dark magic goes against the Lord. You must stop using it."

"I don't mean to," Lilith told him, her small voice shaking as she put her hands out in front of her face, watching the black smoke coming from her palms, "it just comes out. Has the devil really taken me, Daddy?"

"I am not your father," he said quietly, crouching down, his face emerging from the shadows, "the devil is testing us by bringing a demon into this house, he thought we wouldn't notice. But the Lord gives us angels to protect us. Luke showed us your evil."

"I didn't hurt him," Lilith's fear boiled to anger. Her brother died of sickness, he had cancer, she didn't kill him. She didn't touch him. The six-year-old stood so that her face was in line with her father's as he crouched in front of her, black smoke still pouring from her hands, fueled by her anger.

"You killed him," her father's voice shook with rage as tears formed in his eyes, "you murdered my son! With your cancerous witchcraft, you demon."

"If I'm a demon," Lilith told him, tears streaming from her eyes and she clenched her fists together, "why aren't you sick? Why isn't mama sick? Why haven't I hurt you yet?"

"God will protect me and my family from you," her father told her, standing up as he shook his finger in her face, "he loves and protects those who love and worship him."

"God doesn't love me, Daddy," Lilith said, her voice growing quiet as the tips of her fingers began to turn black, corrupting the skin on her hands, travelling slowly to her arms, "not anymore. And he doesn't love you."

"You'll watch your mouth before you speak of the Lord," her father went to grab her by the arm to throw her further into the room, but she pulled away before he could reach her.

"Don't touch me," she screamed at him as she hit her fists to the floor.

Suddenly, brought forth from thin air, a shadowed monster that resembled a gorilla grew in front of him, until it broke through the roof, and glared down at him in the debris. Terrified, Mr. Romano jumped backwards and fell to the ground, staring at the small child that had conjured the beast. His daughter's once white, blonde hair had grown black from the roots, replacing the blonde until only the black remained. Her eyes shone a bright white through the darkness of the smoke that billowed around her.

"Mary," he called, scrambling to his feet, and backing away, "Mary you need to run. The devil has challenged me with the ultimate test, I must fight him."

Mary Romano ran up the stairs, dodging the debris, scared of what she might find. The loud crash had shaken the house, and the roof was destroyed. Looking up, she saw the monster, but that wasn't what scared her the most. The chillingly familiar white eyes of her child made her blood run cold.

"John, don't be an idiot," she told him as her voice shook, her eyes never leaving Lilith, "our daughter is dead, you'll never win against that demon."

Her sudden ability to challenge him shocked him enough to make him turn his head as Lilith lifted her hand towards him. The gorilla let out a deafening roar that echoed throughout the whole town before it began to rampage out of control. It ripped through buildings and anything in its path, leaving Lilith white eyed and alone at the center of the destruction.

The whole town was gone by the time the shadows coursing through her blood reduced enough for her to see what was going on around her. She was more exhausted than she ever had been before, feeling weak as her legs gave out from under her, making her sit in the rubble. She lifted her hand to see her blood-soaked palm from where her monster had ripped her father apart. A small smile formed on her tired face as she closed her hand around his blood, she had got him. She was free of him now.

CHAPTER SIXTEEN
Becoming Mist

"That's freaky," Astor grimaced as he watched Lilith's hand fade into smoke and then reform in front of them both, "that's like all your tissue just...vapourised."

He stared with deep red eyes that were almost brown and littered with golden flecks, dark brown hair fell in curls into his face as he leaned towards the black smoke and reached out to touch it, but Lilith reformed her hand and swatted him away.

"Stop it," she said as she rubbed her thumb along her fingers to put the feeling through her skin that her hand was in fact back in the right place. "You know, you have a fireproof top. You don't have to walk around shirtless all the time."

"But I work so hard to look this good," Astor acted offended as he opened his arms to show off his toned torso, each muscle visible as he flexed at her, only making her frown at him more, "you love it really. Such a hot sidekick like this, we'll have apologists sticking up for us no matter what we do."

Lilith just laughed as he began to stroke his abs, getting to his feet.

His vanity had always been entertaining to her. Sometimes she wasn't entirely sure if he was joking or not, but he seemed to have fun with it.

"Watch this," he said excitedly, giving himself some room as he clenched his fists and brought his arms out sharply to produce flaming wings from his shoulder blades, "cool, right. I need to get someone Italian to paint me. You're Italian right? Paint me?"

"No," Lilith said dryly as footsteps coming from behind made her turn her head to see Emrick coming out to join them.

"What are you doing?" he asked Astor as the fire wielder held his wings as steady as he could.

"Cool, right."

"You look like a demon," Emrick frowned as he watched the flow of fire flicker around the young man's body as he tried to control it.

"Scare the Christians," Astor put on his best gremlin-like voice as he clawed his hands and bounced them forward a little, "I am a demon from hell." Emrick laughed at his joke as he stepped towards where Lilith was sitting.

As he spoke, Astor pumped more power into the wings, making them flare out and almost hit Lilith. In a flinch, Lilith dispersed and became mist, reforming a couple of feet away. There was a second as she held herself steady, then there was a sloshing sound as a portion of her blood volume rematerialized outside her body, hitting the paving stones after it fell.

"I missed," Lilith muttered as she collapsed into Emrick's arms as he rushed forward to catch her, lowering her slowly to the ground.

"You're just a boy," Emrick frowned disapprovingly, his laughter at Astor's joke gone after he saw that Lilith was hurt, "you need to be more careful."

"I'm sorry," he said as he darted forward, his wings gone the second they had gotten too close to Lilith, "I'll take her to her room."

Astor scooped Lilith up from the floor. She was dazed and tired from the blood loss, so she was limp and hard to carry, but she was recovering so she was able to hold onto him a little. He winced slightly as she put her hand on his back, making Emrick take a step behind him and see the burns that retracting his wings so quickly had created.

"It's not that bad," Astor chuckled as he made sure he had Lilith properly held and supported before he started walking, "besides, she needs to rest."

"Get those burns treated, Astor," Emrick told him, frowning at the blisters forming on his back, "please."

"I will," Astor said, watching her head as he took her back into the house through the door, "after I get her to bed."

CHAPTER SEVENTEEN
Channelling

Electricity coursed through Danny's fingers, tingling through his muscle fibers as he held it just under his skin. He was practicing to avoid hurting himself too badly if he messed up. Slowly, he reached his other hand forward and placed it around the metal rod to complete the circuit and make the light bulb glow. He should really be proud that he had done it, but he couldn't bring himself to smile, his worries were taking over his mind and he knew he needed to keep a level head to wield, but nothing could distract him from Lilith. Nothing had succeeded in that for twelve years.

"Danny," Rachel's voice called out to him as he instinctively let go of the metal rods, making a sharp shock go up his arm and hit him in the shoulder, "sorry."

"It's not your fault," Danny sighed, trying to force a smile for her, but it just made him look sadder than before, "I was distracted anyway."

"You did find her then," Rachel smiled gently as she sat down next to him, "your friend."

"Lumin said she was dead," Danny told her, turning in his chair so that he was facing her, "why would he lie to me about that? I feel like he's hiding something from me."

"I wasn't lying," Lumin's voice made him jump at its sudden proximity, he seemed to have an uncanny ability to sneak up on Danny, "I thought she was. She should be. A lot of shadow wielders die young, and power like hers would only corrupt her faster."

"Why?" Danny asked, turning towards him, eagerly awaiting answers to his questions, "what do you mean 'corrupt'? Is Lilith going to die?"

"I don't know, but shadow wielding is corruptive in the sense that the shadow attacks cells," Lumin explained as he sat on the bench next to Rachel, the sleeves of his cable knit jumper pulled halfway over his hands, "It's why most if not all shadow wielders have black hair and fingernails, it affects the keratin in the body first usually. It's also considered carcinogenic, a lot of shadow wielders cause cancers in people around them, purely unintentionally, but mainly in themselves. It's a very dangerous ability to be born with."

Danny looked down at his feet, his brow furrowed as he thought, "Lilith had a little brother, his name was Luke. He died from cancer, was that... did she do that?"

"She wouldn't have been conscious of it," Lumin told him gently, knowing that this was a sensitive subject, "but probably, yes. Though it's also possible her brother was a shadow wielder and did it to himself, or there was someone else in the house. Having young shadow wielders around is difficult because they can't control themselves properly. It's no one's fault, but people tend to get hurt."

"So, she needs help," Rachel said, making Danny lift his head with the ghost of a smile on his face, "if Lilith's in danger while she's out of control, she needs a teacher that'll help her, not a terrorist trying to use her. You're a great teacher, Lumin, she needs you."

"Exactly," Danny shuffled forward on his chair, "we need to help her, let me help her, please."

"I'm not a shadow wielder, I can't teach her something I don't know but, I'm not going to stop you from trying to help someone,"

Lumin said, reaching out and placing a hand on his shoulder, "but I don't want you to go into this assuming that she's going to listen when you try to talk to her. She might try and attack you. I'll try my best to protect you if she does, but I just want you to understand how dangerous she could be."

"I don't want to fight her," Danny's voice shook, his expression filled with torment as he looked at Lumin.

"You might have to," Lumin sighed, giving Danny a pat on the shoulder before pushing on his knees to stand back up. "She might not give you a choice."

"She hasn't done anything wrong," Danny said weakly, looking back down at his feet, "you saw a symbol on her chest, and suddenly she's evil."

"That symbol, it represents a man called Emrick," Lumin explained, turning back towards him, "he's someone with a lot of trauma associated with the Catholic Church, as do many shadow wielders, but instead of helping people overcome that trauma or processing it himself, he has waged war on religion. He has destroyed churches, he doesn't check who's inside, he just destroyed them. The guilty, and the innocent, all the same, all murdered. To him because they love a God that is hateful, they're all guilty."

"I hate that God too," Danny said, his tone a lot colder as he spoke, "does that make me evil?"

"Do you murder children because their parents took them to church?" Lumin asked, frowning at the teenager that sat in front of him. He needed to know that Danny understood the gravity of what they were dealing with.

"No."

"There we are then," Lumin told him, turning back around to leave the room, "not evil. I've known people that hate God and are good people, and I've known people that love God and are bad, I've also known both versions of the opposite. The point is, loving and hating a God makes no difference to who you are, you decide that yourself. Emrick chose to do what he does, just as you are making your choices now."

CHAPTER EIGHTTEEN
Secret Meeting

Black hair held back in a ponytail with two pieces at the front framing her face. Aurora Umbra sat with her feet resting on the table in front of her and her head leant back over the back of her chair, staring at the ceiling above her.

"You know, I heard some interesting news yesterday, you'll never guess what it was," she said, tilting her head down to look at the woman sitting opposite her, "come on Mary, it's no fun if you don't guess."

"I don't know," Mary Romano muttered, her hands pulled firmly into her lap as she tried to avoid eye contact with Aurora, "I haven't heard anything. I don't leave this room."

"No, I suppose you don't," Aurora sighed, taking her feet off the table, and leaning closer to her, "but it turns out Lumin, that electrical wielder, Emrick's...friend, has a new student, a new little electrical wielder. A late bloomer, but he seems strong. Do you know what they call him?"

Mary stayed silent, glancing up occasionally but Aurora had her in an intense stare. Watching to see if Mary would give an indication to the secrets she held tightly inside.

"Danny," Aurora said softly, making Mary's chest tighten, "but there are lots of Dannys around the world, so that's not enough. A friend of mine took a look at his blood, and this part you'll love, my friend said that his blood looks like a lightshow."

Mary's head suddenly snapped up, looking Aurora directly in the eye, heart pounding. Could it be him? Could he help Lilith? No. She couldn't think like that. If it was him, then he would have to keep himself safe from this monster.

"Did you really think you could hide him from me?" Aurora asked with a slight laugh, standing from her chair, and slowly walking around the table as she spoke, "that little block on his energy, did you think, even for a second, that you were stronger than me?"

"No," Mary mumbled, looking down into her lap again as Aurora got closer to her, "I've never thought that."

"Can't even stand up for yourself? God, you're pathetic," Aurora laughed as she leaned down so that she invaded Mary's personal space, her dark eyes burning into the side of Mary's head, "no wonder your daughter tried to kill you. Hiding from a six-year-old, that must have been humiliating."

Trying to flinch away, Mary felt Aurora's hand clasp over her shoulder, pulling her closer to her. The slightly deranged smile on her face terrifying Mary, as Aurora used her other hand to force Mary to look at her.

"But she's a lot bigger now," Aurora smirked, the tips of her fingers digging into Mary's cheeks, "and just down the hall. So don't be too loud when you cry or try to escape, or she'll find you. I've told Lilith not to come in here, so long as she respects that you're safe. Though I am curious to see how she'd kill you, your husband barely had a body left. Such destruction is surely a miracle from the Lord."

Her mocking breath brushed over Mary's cheek, making her flinch and try to pull away as Aurora laughed at her.

"Don't worry," Aurora chuckled, letting go of Mary and standing back up properly, "you know I don't care about Emrick's little war on religion, but whatever keeps him motivated. You're not a traitor to me. Allowing a non-wielder to try and suppress the powers of a wielder though, that did make me disappointed in you."

"I'm sorry, I just-" Mary started, but Aurora waved her to silence as she sat back down.

"You were afraid of him, I understand," Aurora said softly, tilting her head as she continued to stare at Mary, "if you hadn't been hiding from me at the time, I would've been able to show you how much stronger you were than him. It's basic biology. Evolution; the strong live, and the weak die. Those born without the advantage are useless, and don't deserve to survive."

Mary looked as though she was trying to bite back her tongue, but she ended up bringing forth the courage to reply. "You won't succeed. She won't let you."

"Ashido's not going to save you," Aurora laughed, standing from her chair, and turning towards the door, "she doesn't care. If anything, I think she agrees with me."

"But she hates you," Mary's voice shook as she held her ground against Aurora.

"Shut up," Aurora spat harshly, her sudden change in tone making Mary retreat instantly, "Ashido won't leave her mountain and you will never leave my side again. There is no use in pissing me off."
Aurora crossed the room and closed the door behind her as she left, leaving Mary sitting alone in the room she couldn't leave without risking her life. She had been hiding for longer than she hadn't been, firstly from Aurora and now from her own daughter. Her cage was comfortable, and she didn't want to leave it.

CHAPTER NINETEEN
Checking In

Slowly, Lilith's eyes fluttered open to see the worried look on Astor's face as he glanced over at her, seemingly in reflex because he had turned away from her again before he realised that she was looking at him. He quickly spun back around in the armchair to double check if he had seen it correctly.

"Hello," he said quietly, so as not to bother her as she came around, "welcome back."

"Thank you," Lilith's voice was hoarse as she pushed herself up in the bed, propping herself up with some pillows.

"You shouldn't be doing that so casually," Emrick told her, making her turn her head to see where he had come from. He was standing in the doorway, his arms folded as he watched her. "You'll lose more than just blood if you're not more careful."

"Aurora says it's good to practice like that," Lilith said with a slight smirk. Going over his head was one of her favourite ways to wind him up, she had a feeling he didn't like having a boss. "She uses it all the time."

"Aurora has a lot more control over herself, and her gift, than you, or I, do," Emrick smiled back at her, she was too tired to hide her schemes from him, "and we're partners in this, she isn't my boss. Astor, will you leave us for a moment, please."

Astor gave a courteous nod as he stood from his chair, turning back to look at Lilith as he left the room, "Ooh, you're in trouble."

Emrick laughed as he walked over and sat on the bed next to her, "You're not in trouble, don't worry about that. I need to ask you something. Do you know a boy named Daniel Andrews?"

"What about him?" Lilith asked, shuffling to sit up more so that she wasn't so slouched. The muscle in her jaw tightened.

"That third student, the one you weren't expecting," Emrick watched her frown as she worked out where he was going with it, "that was Daniel Andrews."

"Wha- Why would he be with them?" Lilith asked him, leaning forward as her heart began to beat a little faster. "That doesn't make any sense."

"How did you know him?" Emrick asked, standing as he began to pace around her room, "what was your relationship with him?"

"Don't dodge the question," Lilith frowned, following him with her eyes as he went to stand by the window.

"He's an electrical wielder," Emrick said quickly, hoping that she wouldn't dwell on the comment, "how did you know him?"

"No, he's not," Lilith watched Emrick intently as he stared out into the trees that hid the edge of the city from view, "he would have told me when we were kids."

"Lilith," Emrick said, turning to face her again, "answer the question."

"He was my friend," she told him, her frown a little deeper than usual.

"Did you love him?"

"I was six, I didn't know what love was."

"Do you love him now?" Emrick watched her closely as she stared back at him, her face barely moving as she gave little to no reaction.

"I don't know him now," she told him, her eyes finally breaking her stare as she pulled the covers off of her legs to get out of the bed.

"Will you have a problem fighting him?" Emrick asked as she stood from the bed, only turning her head to look back at him, "Will you hesitate?"

"If he gets in my way," Lilith shrugged, walking towards the door, "then he's just another traitor."

She went through the door, leaving Emrick standing at the window. He wanted to trust that she would be able to see past her feelings, but she was a very emotional person, even if she didn't show it all the time. His fear that she would be distracted and get herself killed sat in his chest like a lead weight. He knew that if it were him, and he had to fight her, he would hesitate. She was meant to be nothing more than a weapon, but he had raised her, and he couldn't see past that.

CHAPTER TWENTY
Dark Past

Fern could feel Danny's eyes on the back of her head, but she didn't want to answer his questions. They weren't secrets she wanted to tell, but they both knew that Lumin would just avoid the truth if he asked. She heard him stand from his perch on the counter and walk over to her. He sat on the chair next to hers at the dining room table, watching to see if she was ignoring him on purpose.

"How long have you known Lumin?" he asked, breaking the silence finally.

"A very long time," she told him simply, not looking up from her laptop as she kept typing away.

"How does he know Lilith?" Danny asked, almost forcing the question from his mouth. He had been terrified to speak it out loud and even as the words left his mouth, he could feel his heart beating hard in his chest.

Fern paused. Silence reigned as she stopped typing. "He doesn't," was all she said before going back to whatever she was doing on her computer.

"You're a worse liar than he is," Danny snapped, his fist clenched on his leg as he stared at her while she refused to look at him, "I don't know you that well, which is why I feel like I can be harsher with you when I ask my questions. I have no reason to spare your feelings because I have no way of telling how you're going to react to what I say."

Finally, Fern stopped what she was doing and turned her head towards Danny. "He doesn't know her."

"Has he met her before?" Danny leant forward in desperation, not wanting to miss anything. He felt like he would explode if he didn't move, his whole body felt electrified, but at the same time he felt frozen to his seat, almost paralysed.

"Yes, he has met her before," Fern told him, closing the laptop, and turning towards him.

"Why didn't he tell me?"

"Because it's none of your business," Fern said harshly, frowning at his boldness as she picked up her laptop, "and it isn't any of mine either, so if you want to know more than that then you need to ask him about it. If he wants to, he'll tell you."

Feeling the frustration building, Danny focused on forcing it down instead of arguing with her, letting her leave the room in silence.

A soft knock on Lumin's bedroom door made him look up from his book and wait for someone to speak or knock for a second time. When the second knock came, Lumin stood from the bed and walked to the door, opening it to find Danny waiting outside.

"Can I talk to you?" he asked, a slight furrow in his brow as he looked up at his teacher, "about the time you met Lilith."

Lumin's head tilted a little as he looked at the determined look on the boy's face. There was no use lying to him, he was clearly sure of himself. "Come in."

Danny followed Lumin into his room. He pulled the chair out from his desk, letting Danny sit on the bed.

"How much do you know about it?" Lumin asked, leaning his forearms on the back of the chair as he sat on it the wrong way round.

"That you've met her before," Danny said, shuffling a little as he sat, "and that apparently it's none of my business even though she had been my only proper friend until very recently, and you knew that, and you know that I want to find her to help her."

"You spoke to Fern," Lumin chuckled, knowing how Fern would have spoken to Danny, "she can be a little closed off sometimes. Did you catch her while she was working?"

"I think so," Danny told him, looking down at his hands as he tried to relax.

"Yeah, I'm pretty sure she keeps a gardening blog," Lumin said, a thoughtful look on his face as he spoke, "but she won't tell me the name of it. I don't know why she's so embarrassed, I only wanted to support her, I'm sure it's very interesting."

"Lumin," Danny said, trying to bring him back to the point of the conversation. "We were talking about Lilith?"

"Right, sorry," Lumin smiled weakly and looked down to avoid eye contact with Danny, "I'm a little nervous to tell you this if I'm honest. I'm not very proud of this part of my past."

"It's okay, Lumin," Danny reassured him, "I just want to know what happened to my friend."

"Okay, so when I was younger, I was...uh... good friends with Emrick, before he became a terrorist," Lumin explained, making Danny raise his eyebrows in surprise, "we got on well. He always believed wielders should be more open about themselves, and their gifts. Which I agreed with and to an extent I still do. I wish we could be more open about who we are without being outcast, hated or experimented on, but people get scared when faced with things they don't understand."

Danny nodded as he listened, making sure not to interrupt Lumin as he told him the story.

"Twelve years ago, we heard about the incident with Lilith," he continued, "Emrick became fixated on her as an example of the treatment of shadow wielders. You see, because it's so dangerous, shadow wielders tend to be taught how to suppress their abilities and never use them again, but Emrick thought that that was ridiculous. He wanted them to be taught how to use their gifts fully."

"What did he do?" Danny asked, shuffling forward on the bed as he listened.

"Eight years ago, Emrick, Fern and I went to the Shadow Wielding Facility for Orphaned Youth and took Lilith so that she could be properly trained," Lumin told him, his eyes firmly looking down at the floor.

"You kidnapped her," Danny frowned as he leaned away from Lumin, "from a place where she was safe?"

"From a place that would have killed her," Lumin defended himself as he snapped his head back up to look Danny in the eye for a moment before looking away again, "you can't suppress power like that without hurting her. But yes, we kidnapped her."

"What happened?" Danny asked, his glare burning from his eyes as he watched the guilty expression on Lumin's face, "why didn't you stay with her?"

"When she told us about what happened to her," Lumin went on to continue his story, "the abuse, and the involvement of the local church, Emrick was furious. It made him spiral down this path of revenge against Christians at first, but I don't think he'd care now as long as they believe in that God. Emrick also has a history of abuse at the hands of people that used God as an excuse to hurt him, it hit home for him. He became obsessed, and I wasn't going to follow him down a path that could lead to genocide. Neither was Fern. Lilith wouldn't leave his side. She trusted him the most out of all of us."

Danny was quiet for a moment, thinking over what he had been told. "Why did you think she was dead, if you knew where she was?"

"I didn't think he could succeed. I thought he would push her too hard, and she would end up killing herself by accident, or" Lumin explained, using his hands to better explain himself, "there's something that can happen to shadow wielders called complete corruption. In this state, the shadow takes over the body, their blood runs black. So, their eyes are black, any cuts they have bleed black, their skin has a dark grey tint to it. It's disturbing to see, and they are overrun with power at that point. I've never known of a shadow wielder to survive it. I was surprised it didn't happen to her during that first incident when she was a child."

"Is that everything?" Danny asked quietly, standing from the bed, and turning away from Lumin, "you're not keeping anything else from me?"

"No," Lumin said softly, glancing up at him briefly to watch him leave the room.

CHAPTER TWENTY-ONE
Getting Started

As she walked down the hallway, Lilith spotted Astor with his ear pressed against one of the doors. It was the one they weren't allowed into, which made Lilith frown at his stupidity.

"What are you doing?" she asked, causing him to jump away from the door and quickly turn to face her.

"Oh, it's you," he sighed, leaning back against the door, "you've gotta be curious about what she keeps in here too, right? One room in the whole house that we're not allowed in, always locked. It's weird."

"No," Lilith batted at his face with her hand to get him away from the door that was covered in black runes, "I'm not. I don't care what's behind there, it's nothing to do with us. And you shouldn't be so nosey into Aurora's things, it's like you like being choked on smoke."

"Only yours, darling," he smirked, leaning down towards her glaring expression as she backed away from him.

"Astor!"

"Yes sir," Astor snapped back to standing almost immediately like someone had pressed a button on a remote to control him.

"Don't be so vulgar," Emrick snapped at him, walking up behind Lilith with a light frown on his face, "get away from the door, both of you, before Aurora sees you."

"Sorry sir," Astor gave an awkward half bow before turning and walking quickly away from the two of them, down the stairs and out of sight.

"I have this feeling that he's making fun of me," Emrick sighed as he turned back to Lilith.

"Who? Astor?" she said sarcastically as she began to follow the fire wielder down the stairs, "no, he would never."

Emrick chuckled before he began to walk away from the door himself, "Lilith, wait, I have a surprise for you and Astor."

"What is it?" she asked, not stopping as they walked down the stairs together to join Astor, who was waiting at the bottom to try and scare them.

"You two will be making our first move very soon," he smiled as Astor jumped out from behind the bannister and huffed as he gained no reaction from either of them, "a church in Maine called the police last night because a child walked into the church producing 'the devil's fire' from their hands. Originally the police thought it was a joke, but when they got there, part of the church was on fire and the kid was still there and crying. They arrested him for arson, but we know better. That child went looking for help from God, and they turned him away."

"Let's kill them," Lilith smiled, turning to Astor who had a deep glare on his face, "don't worry, I'll let you burn it down."

"Thank you," he said quietly, memories of his past running through his head as he thought about the little boy who sat in a cell for a fire he didn't mean to set. "I'll burn them all to ash."

"You're a good boy Astor," Emrick told him, placing a comforting hand on his shoulder as he made sure that he was okay before he went out on a mission, "Aurora and I are going to go and check on the kid, offer to train him if you're up for it."

"I'd be honoured," Astor forced a smile through the tears that threatened his eyes, "I'll make sure he's strong and free in his own power."

"I know I'm hard on you," Emrick sighed, smiling at him as he let go of his shoulder and let him follow Lilith, "but you do make me proud with how far you've come."

"Thanks Rick," Astor changed his tune to a cheerier one that made Emrick laugh as he held out a thumbs up to him as he reached the door, "I'll be a great teacher, just you wait and see."

CHAPTER TWENTY-TWO
An Attack On Maine

The steady sound of his breathing filled his ears as he sat with his legs crossed, one hand held just in front of Dex's as he mirrored Danny's position, the other with his little finger extended to join the circuit with Dex. The electricity flowed through the two of them steadily as Danny's hand began to itch a little.

"Focus," Dex told him, his brow furrowed as he kept his eyes closed. If Danny messed up now, he would hurt them both.

"I'm trying," Danny snapped back at him, the irritation in his hand making his fingers twitch, "this is really hard."

With a sigh, Dex removed his charge from the circuit, letting Danny's electrical energy bounce back and hit him in the hand. Danny yelped as he got zapped by his own electricity again, falling onto his back as he clutched at his cramping hand.

"You did that on purpose," he moaned as he sat back up.

"You were gonna burn me," Dex said, standing up from the floor and dusting himself off as Fern came and knelt beside Danny.

"Was not," Danny huffed as Fern took his hand and wrapped it in a strangely wet leaf, "ugh! What is that?"

"It's going to heal your burn, it's a special anti-burn plant," she smiled at him softly as she wrapped her hands around the leaf to increase the healing properties of the plant. "You see if Lumin wasn't such a shut in, then you guys wouldn't have so many scars."

"Is it one of your own invention?" Danny asked, looking closely at the clear gel that was oozing out of the sides, "is it going to glow?"

"No, it won't glow," Fern told him, removing her hands, and peeling off the leaf before she wiped off the gel left on his healed hand, "and I didn't invent it, this is aloe vera. I just help it work faster."

"Oh," Danny sighed as Lumin came crashing into the room, making everyone turn to look at him in confusion.

"He's made a move," he panted, holding onto the door frame, "Emrick. He's attacking a church. One of the people inside called the police, they said there was a man who could make fire with his hands and a woman that was being followed around by a dog made of black smoke. She's there."

"Lilith?" Fern asked, her voice shaking as she watched his face intently, only when he nodded, did she let out her sigh of relief.

"Then we've gotta go and get her," Danny said with a determined look on his face, standing up from the floor with a jump.

"We've got to take her out," Dex's tone was more serious than usual, gaining him a glare from Danny, "she's going to kill a church full of people, you wanna go and just say hey why don't you come play house with me? She's not going to listen to you."

"I have to try," Danny's glare softened as he tried to convince himself that this would go smoothly, but if he was honest with himself, he couldn't see this ending without a fight.

To keep everyone inside, Lilith had left the church to keep an eye on the exits. She stood beside her wolf with her back leaning against the big doors at the front of the church. As she stared up at the clouds that sat amongst the blue sky, the door opened next to her, making her turn to see Astor ushering a group of kids out of the church.

"What are you doing?" she asked, glancing between the clearly terrified children and Astor.

"You want to kill the kids too?" he asked with a confused frown as he pushed the littlest one out into the open air.

"You're too soft," Lilith sighed as she turned to the kids and bent down to their height, "God is dead, and He always hated you. Run away orphans."

"Are you serious?" Astor asked her as they watched the kids run away from the church, giving small screams as they went.

"Lili!" the sound of his voice made both their heads turn. Astor waited for her to do something, but she seemed to just accept the shortening of her name.

"Oh, he can call you Lili," Astor scoffed as straightened himself up properly, ready to fight, "precious Daniel can call you Lili, not your best friend Astor. You're Lilith to Astor who has stuck by your side all this time."

"Shut your mouth and burn the church," she snapped at him, dispersing the wolf, and bringing her hands back into the shape of the dog shadow puppet, "I'll keep them off your back."

"Please, I just wanna talk to you," Danny pleaded with her, edging closer as she watched him step ahead of the other three, "I don't wanna fight you."

"Are you here to help?" she asked, a soft smile on her face as Astor disappeared back into the church, closing the door behind him.

"No," he shook his head, a painful look on his face as he watched the woman he no longer knew.

"Then we don't really need to talk then do we."

CHAPTER TWENTY-THREE
Four VS One

In under a second, Lilith tilted her hands forward, morphing her shadow wolf into its larger form, then quickly moved her hands into a bird shape. With a flick of her hands, the shadow bird cawed and followed her command as she sent it to her left. Almost hitting Amelia in the chest, but she just about managed to dodge it.

"Where do you think you're going?" Lilith asked, her stare intense as she locked eyes with the electrical wielder, "you don't want to get caught in the fire, do you?"

"I won't let you kill these people," Amelia glared as she got ready to fight her, her hands charged up like a taser.

Lilith laughed as fire burst through the stained-glass windows, Astor had begun to incinerate the church, "you're too late. Those people are already dead."

A spark caught Lilith's eye through the smoke. In an instant, she became mist. Dex dashed through her, hitting hard into the door. Reforming herself, Lilith simply smirked at his bewildered expression as her head turned back to look at him.

Time seemed to pause as she looked at him. Barely an arm's length away, Dex could feel his hands shaking as they froze in a stand still.

"Dex!" Lumin shouted in fear as the wolf began to disappear as her attention wavered off of it, "get away from her, now!"

Following his orders, Dex made a dash for Amelia. Picking her up, he took them both away from the shadow wielder. Becoming mist was supposed to be incredibly difficult and the risk to life was immense. To use it to dodge - Lilith was either crazy or much more powerful than they thought, or both.

"So, you wanna fight me now," Lilith said, turning towards Lumin as he pushed Danny behind his shoulder, "what happened to the man that told me everything was going to be okay and that I was safe with him?"

"He watched you become a killer," Lumin said darkly, hitting his hands together with a painful grunt, and sending streams of electricity through the air.

Lilith infused her legs with her energy, allowing her to jump over the current and form wings to glide up into the air. Gracefully, she dispersed them and fell into her shadow bird, letting it carry her over the top of them.

"I can do this," Danny muttered to himself as he tried to keep eyes on the bird, psyching himself up so that he would be able to throw a punch, "I can fight her. She's going down."

"You'll die," Lumin told him firmly, glancing back slightly, "don't try it. I want you to run. Find Amelia and Dex and get yourselves away from here."

With a deep frown of concentration, Lumin hit his fists together again, sending another charge up towards the bird, electrifying the smoke. Trying to see through the falling cloud, Lumin was too late to see Lilith coming down with a kick to Danny's head. He slammed into the ground, blood beginning to pour down his face as she stood over him.

"Do you think I'll get one of you today?" Lilith asked, looking down at Danny as he pushed himself back to his feet as fast as he could, a sick smile on her face.

"Shut up," Lumin yelled, throwing a hard punch her way, only for her to become mist again and reform behind him.

Blood dripped from her hand as she stood laughing maniacally. She didn't seem like the girl he remembered, Lumin thought as he watched her. Something didn't feel right. The church burned brightly through the smoke as Astor reappeared through the door, a little singed across his cheeks as he turned back to close the door behind him.

"You're gonna hurt yourself Lili," Danny said, charging up his hands as calmly as he could, but he could feel his skin itching.

"If I get to take out one of you wannabe heroes," she said quietly, watching Astor torch the outside of the building before turning back to him, "then it'll be worth it."

"Why did you change so much?" he asked, looking at her with tears forming in his eyes as the electricity in his hands began to burn his skin.

"Because it's what people do," she told him simply, turning back to Lumin. Knowing he wasn't a threat to her; she would mostly ignore him. "You should try it."

With her eyes fixed on her former guardian, Lilith brought her hand to her lips. With her thumb and pinkie finger extended, her eyes flicked over to where Amelia and Dex were watching, and she lifted her hand. As soon as her head tilted back, Amelia began to grasp at her throat, her mouth filling with black shadow, choking her as she fell to her knees.

Lumin swung forward again, but this time Lilith didn't block his attack. Astor did. A strong stream of fire shot towards him as Lilith ducked out of the way of the flame. Trying to help, Danny lunged forward to try and get Lilith to let Amelia go, but she knocked him back easily and stood to get above him again after Astor finished attacking Lumin to see if he had killed him.

"Just sit this one out," she told Danny harshly, "you're clearly not skilled enough to even try. You shouldn't be here."

"But I've been practicing," Danny smiled with determination as he lashed out hard, just about catching her in the chest with a charge of electricity that went through her whole body, knocking her back into Astor.

The burning sensation was enough to break her concentration on Amelia, and the shadow stopped choking her. Dex checked that she was okay before he took a dash at their two enemies. With his speed amplified like that, Astor had no hope of dodging, and he wasn't fast enough to take a shot at him. Dex hit Astor in the arm, knocking it out of its socket as he flew across the street, leaving Lilith standing alone, clutching her side, in front of Dex.

With a slight frown on her face, Lilith reached out towards him, her hand open in front of her. She seemed to stare at the tips of her fingers as she went to touch him.

"Dex run!" Lumin coughed as he tried to sit up with the burns on his arms, face, and chest ripping at his skin. His whole body aching with pain.

As fast as he could, Dex launched himself back before Lilith could get to him. Her fingertips just brushed the front of his suit, but he was too fast for her to do anything. Like a blur, he zipped around her to pick up Lumin and Danny and bring them over to where Amelia was trying to catch her breath. The raw pain and the taste of blood in her throat made it difficult to breathe.

"I need you to carry Amelia," Dex ordered Danny as he put all his remaining energy into lifting Lumin, "I can't do both. Put your wielding into your legs, you'll go faster."

Once he had a proper hold on Lumin, Dex glanced over at Lilith, who looked slightly dazed, before zipping off to get his teacher away from the fight.

"I've got you," Danny grunted, lifting Amelia from the floor as she continued to draw sharp and shaky breaths that sounded painful. With everything he had left, he channelled his electricity into his legs, making them tense up a little, and then took off in the same direction as Dex.

Black spots forming in her vision, Lilith watched as the electrical wielders fled. "How disappointing," she muttered as she began to sway, trying to keep herself upright.

"How're you doing there, sailor?" Astor asked, grunting a little from the pain in his shoulder.

Lilith didn't answer for a moment and then fell back into his good arm, which caught her immediately. "Feeling great. Too bad we didn't get at least one of them though."

"Don't worry," Astor smiled, resting his head on top of hers, "they'll be there for the next church, they're annoying like that. How's your hand?"

"Bit missing," Lilith chuckled sleepily, as she lifted up her right hand, letting the blood dripping out of her ring finger flow down her arm, "I lost the tip."

Astor brought his good hand around her shoulder and placed her stubbed finger into his palm so that he could cauterise the wound. She winced but tried not to flinch, grateful that she didn't bleed out in the street while they waited for Emrick to come and get them. Astor couldn't carry her the way he was, and she couldn't walk after all the blood she had lost while becoming mist. They had no choice but to sit and wait.

CHAPTER TWENTY-FOUR
Within The Darkness

Lilith Romano sat in the garden of Emrick's estate, breathing in the open air with her hands resting in her lap.

"A whole tip of your finger, yikes," Aurora laughed as she sat next to Lilith on the bench, "blood is hard, I get that, all those capillaries. I used to get bruises all the time. But a piece of your finger, and you lost it, that's forever."

"I am aware," Lilith sighed, looking over at her usual smug smirk.

"Don't look so down," Aurora chuckled, hitting her in the arm, "the world isn't that dark, not yet."

"This world is hell, Aurora." Lilith told her, "There is darkness everywhere. So, there is no reason why I can't hide within its darkness."

Danny sat on the floor with his back to the wall and his knees pulled up to his chest, staring straight at the floor. After getting back to Lumin's Wielding Academy, they had all needed treatment from Fern, but his burns weren't too bad, and he hadn't worn down his energy completely, so he just tried to stay out of the way. He could hear Rachel speaking, but he didn't want to move from where he was. Nothing felt real as he hid in his little corner.

"He's okay," Dex said to Rachel, looking up at her with a little sparkle in his eye. He couldn't move from his seat now that the energy had left his legs, so he was glad that she had come to see him. "He did good too and he didn't back down."

"Thank you, Dex," Rachel smiled, ruffling his hair a little as she looked over at Danny, who had finally looked up from the floor.

He saw, for what he was pretty sure the first time, Dex smile. Dex didn't take his eyes off Rachel who gave a sort of half-hearted knowing smile back, which made Danny feel a little sorry for him, but he had to sympathise with Rachel as well. After all, he was just a kid. She stood up and made her way over to Danny.

"Are you okay?" she asked, a concerned frown on her face as she placed a hand on his shoulder.

"I couldn't do anything," he told her, tears forming in his eyes as he tried to get the words out in the right order, "I was completely useless out there. I can't hold back against her, but I don't want to hurt her either. She's a murderer, and I still don't hate her. What's wrong with me?"

"Hey," Fern said, reaching down to grab his cheek and pull his face to make him look at her, "you saved Amelia's life, you weren't useless. You did extremely well, considering the circumstances, no one else got a hit on her. She underestimated you, and you used it to your advantage, that's smart."

"Be proud of yourself Danny," Lumin said groggily, wincing a little as he lifted his head from the bed, "you gave it your best. The world is a dark place, but it won't be forever."

"This world is hell. There is darkness everywhere. So, there is no reason why I can't be a light in that darkness," Danny's face held a deep glare of concentration as they all watched him, "I will save her Lumin. I promise."

AUTHOR'S NOTE

Hi, you're at the end. So, one of two things has happened; you have flipped to the end to read this, in which case hello, my name is Morgan Barnard, I wrote the book you're holding. The other option is that you have just finished Wielder Volume one, in which case, thank you and I hope you enjoyed this story as much as I did making it.

For those of you that have read the book, here is a fun little fact about it:

Fern does have a gardening blog which she posts on every day, she thinks that Lumin would make fun of her for it because she's a plant wielder and even she finds it cliché, even so it's quite popular and has a lot of readers.

Printed in Great Britain
by Amazon

85082778R00063